To Lovely Anne,

Never undere[stimate]...

Much Love,

Joanna
xxxx

Benchmark

Joanna Louise Wright

Copyright © 2015 Joanna Louise Wright

All rights reserved.

ISBN-10 1514115905
ISBN: 13 978-1514115909

DEDICATION

To the two amazing people who inspired me to raise my game,

Never underestimate how much I love you.

Always,

xxxx Mum xxxx

ACKNOWLEDGEMENTS

People say that reading a book can change you as a person. I never imagined that writing a book would have the same effect. It started off as a goal on a wish list of things I'd love to do. I did not believe that I could actually do it because a) I am not a literary genius and b) I had no idea what I was doing! I read an article in Psychologies Magazine in 2011 that encouraged people to spend 30 minutes a day, working on a dream, to move it forward. I bought a notebook and decided to give it a try.

That was the start of an incredible personal adventure, one which has taught me so much about myself. I've learnt that doing a little something every day can build such momentum that eventually you realise you are actually achieving your dream; that feeling of joy is wonderful. I've also developed the ability to learn on the job, take each hurdle as it comes and find ways to jump over them. I've learnt that I love the process of writing and letting myself get lost on paper for hours on end. I've also learnt a lot about procrastination, how to break through it and in turn I've become self-disciplined and focused.

One of the most wonderful things about writing this book has been collaborating with my talented illustrator Patricia Lewis. We had numerous 'Tea and Toast' meetings to discuss ideas and develop them whilst also talking about life, the universe and everything! I would like to thank Pat for her sparkling talent and for sharing this adventure with me.

I would also like to give huge thanks to my typist and grammar expert, Sioux Richardson (a.k.a. Mum). Her enthusiasm to help has been unwavering and invaluable. I'd actually forgotten that semi-colons existed so I will be eternally grateful that she re-introduced them to me; they are quite useful! Thank you also to Sioux for all the help during the painstaking editing process. "Is this in the right tense?". "Hold on, I've started the sentence with a big But!" You have been amazing, thank you.

I'd also like to thank my two fantastic sons, Harvey and Ronan, for supporting me from the start and encouraging me with hugs, pats on the back and kisses on the head at all the important milestones along the way. I love you with all my heart.

Thank you to my amazing network of people who kept me afloat in the difficult days and who share the sunshine on the happy days. I treasure you all: 'The Classy Ladies', 'Team Cooke, Team Murtagh, Team Lewis, Team Gasowski, Team Wilkinson', 'The Carlo Rossi Army', 'The Caversham Dining Club', 'WSD Family', 'WW Family' 'EPC Buddies' and all my special friends, you know who you are. Thank you also to my wonderful supportive man, Darren, who encourages me in all I do and has shown me what real and true love is. Thank you also to my lovely family. I love you all.

Massive thanks to everyone who has encouraged me along the way. There are hundreds of you. Every positive comment has spurred me on. It really has helped. Thank you also to my first readers, who have given me their feedback, spotted errors and written some wonderful reviews.

A big thank you to Michael Heppell Ltd for letting me use his book title 'How to Be Brilliant' in the story. I read this when I was 30. It helped turn my life around and was my first step on the Self-Development Ladder, I truly recommend it. Thank you also to the endless list of Personal Development Authors/Speakers who have inspired me to improve my mind, character, personal growth and taught me so much about how to live an authentically happy, fulfilled and positive life. I'm still learning and I love it! My favourites: John C Maxwell, Brendon Burchard, Michael Heppell, Jim Rohn, Darren Hardy, Elizabeth Gilbert and Tony Wrighton... to name but a few.

Thank you also to "Google". At every hurdle in my journey, I was able to say, "I'll Google it" and there at my fingertips were hundreds of helpful articles to help me. Thank you also to Createspace who have made it so straightforward to self-publish my own work.

Also, thank you to Alana Leevy, my protagonist. I've spent a lot of time with her over the last 3 years and I love her because she set me free.

Lastly, thank you to you, for taking the time to read the story that I wanted to tell; perhaps, needed to tell. I hope you enjoy it.

Never underestimate setting off on a wonderful adventure.

Much love,
Joanna Louise Wright

INTRODUCTION

I cannot determine whether my life would have been easier had I never had that first encounter with him. From that very first day, he became the Benchmark on which I would base all my future feelings and judgements of men. In fact, it was not so much about him but more about how I felt in his company.

> *"There is no better me than when I am with you*
> *Relaxed, content, alive, electrified*
> *Life coloured in."*

How different my life could have been without that nagging little voice in my head, "He is not Ben". How much more open and receptive could I have been had I not been yearning to feel that 'Ben' feeling? That magic. Would I have been happier in those moments and treated them with more care?

It is interesting to me that, out of the hundreds of people I have encountered on my journey through life so far, I have not found another human being, man or woman, whom I have connected with in the same way. Don't get me wrong, I have an amazing best friend, who is more like a little sister (just one month littler!), whom I can talk to about anything and everything. I have great relationships with men and women alike; strong and true friendships. I open up to people, talk and listen to everyone and love communicating. It is just that this one man has the ability to live inside my brain 24 hours a day, 7 days a week with the odd holiday here and there, when I am determined to combat his internal squatting. But somehow, he always makes his return when I am least expecting it.

> *"There is only you that reoccurs*
> *So what am I to do?*
> *No matter who or what or why*
> *It all comes back to you."*

I am imagining that had things been different, this intensity and depth of feeling would have been a good thing; probably, true love in its truest form. A lot is written about love; libraries of literature about couples taking forever to unite but getting there eventually. What are they called? Ah, yes, 'happy endings'. Not only books about the subject but films, too: 'Bridget Jones'; 'Notting Hill' and 'The Sound of Music' etc. They are bitter-sweet to read and watch; sweet, because I genuinely feel happy for these fictional characters who open a window of hope in my heart for a few days but bitter, because it is almost definitely a fact that this will not be happening to me.

So, this is a little tale about love that I need to tell just because it's true. If it does not get put onto paper and read, then it will be an even bigger waste than it is now. It will not get snapped up by Universal Studios as the blockbuster of the century, due to the omission of the happy ending but, nevertheless, that will not deter me from my quest to write this man out of my head, not out of my life, but out of my head.

> *"There is nothing to draw me near*
> *No hope or dream exists*
> *And yet you wander through my mind in multiplying twists."*

The multiplying twists are a real issue. So let's go back to the beginning and try to establish when, where and how it all began.

Never underestimate getting yourself into a big, tangled mess.

CHAPTER 1

The Wedding

It was a sunny day, ten years ago. I arrived at the church in my reliable relic of a Fiesta and was instantly acutely aware that my little car was the oldest, rustiest and dirtiest vehicle in the entire car park. I had bought a new dress for the occasion, fitted in all the right places, and I was feeling relatively good.

I stepped out of the car and onto the gravel, which was not ideal for the heels I was wearing! I hobbled across to the entrance of the grand church and was relieved to be on firm ground again. As I looked up, a man in an immaculate, grey morning suit, with a perfect white shirt and cream cravat had clocked my relief and gave a wry smile. It was a smile that lasted just seconds before he was whisked away inside by the groom. But that smile was it. That was the simple little seed planted; a smile lasting a mere three seconds that said "In this very moment, I get you".

I entered the church and only then did I feel slightly alone. It had not occurred to me to want company until that moment. I'd met a few people before at gatherings of the happy couple but at that moment in time, I could see no-one familiar.

Eventually, I decided to take a seat five rows back, on the bride's side, an aisle seat. A family with two small children sat beside me and apologised for the noise in advance. Fortunately, with two small children of my own, at least they had found themselves next to a compassionate and sympathetic person, unlike the miserable old one behind me who kept huffing and puffing when the youngest child started singing 'Bob the Builder' during the bride's entrance. I agreed, it was bad timing but it was quite humorous. Indeed, I was smiling to myself when I turned to look at the beautiful bride. Simultaneously, the immaculately dressed best man had turned around to check out the little singer. Once again, our eyes met in a brief moment, both having smiled at the same time, at the same thing. In a flash, it was gone again but for the rest of the ceremony I had lost concentration. Who was that man? Where was his wife? I racked my brain to try to remember the important details that Jenna had been so excited to tell me in an email months ago. Who did she say was Michael's best man?

The two little angels next to me even started to grate on my nerves eventually and I heard myself tut and sigh. Then it hit me. The best man was Ben Rutherford, the bride's imminent brother-in-law. He was Michael's brother. Now it made sense. I had heard Jenna talk of Michael's charming older brother; very well educated, at Oxford no less, and now an exceptionally successful barrister. I looked again at his suit, the way he stood so strong, proud and confident. I suddenly felt a lot less sure of myself and looked around the church again, longing to find a friendly face. Aha – Lucy. She gave me a warm wave and I felt better. The service lasted what seemed like forever. I made a conscious effort to look away from the back of Ben Rutherford's head.

After the ceremony, I found Lucy and we exchanged the usual "long time no see" chatter and headed for the reception next door.

It was a long, lovely wedding day filled with delicious food, cake and varied company. The reception party in the evening came alive with dancing and laughter and it was great to see Jenna and Michael so gloriously happy, surrounded by their favourite people.

Throughout the evening, my eyes were drawn increasingly often to Ben. We had been at opposite ends of the dance floor for some time but I observed that he was a popular man, not afraid to show off his best moves after a beer or two. Interestingly, there appeared to be no 'Mrs Ben Rutherford' at his side.

I could tell it was getting late; my feet were starting to ache from the incessant dancing in my ridiculous heels. I chose to leave the dance floor and finally made the sensible decision to exchange wine for water. As I sat at the bar, I realised Ben was approaching with an older couple. I glanced across at them and smiled. Ben smiled back and I felt a shyness wash over me that I was not used to. I ordered my water and couldn't help but listen in to the conversation beside me. I soon realised the couple were Ben and Michael's parents.

As the conversation ended, the couple headed upstairs. Perhaps they'd had enough of the thumping music and were retiring to their room. I was quite looking forward to retiring to mine; my feet were at burning stage, even when I was sitting down.

Eventually, my water arrived and Ben smiled over at me. He pointed to my glass, "That looks like a sensible idea!".
   "Mmm, yes, sensible, but not very appealing", I replied, frowning at my glass of water. Ben laughed and sat on the bar stool beside me.
   "How about a nightcap? My treat." He gestured to the barman, who seemed to instinctively know what he wanted. I smiled

mischievously and nodded, "Well, that sounds like a much better idea!" Ben smiled across at me and said to the barman, "Make that two."

To this day, I do not know what that drink was but it made our conversation flow. It made me amiable and funny at the right times. We sat at the bar, just the two of us, for quite some time. We swapped very brief life stories and as I sat there and heard myself say out loud that I was "a single parent, not working at the moment as I had my hands full", I realised how starkly different our worlds were. But it didn't seem to matter. We talked about sport, the wedding guests, the manor house etc. A while later, the party ended and guests filtered through to the bar area to disrupt the magical moment in time. Ben stood up and offered his hand to help me hop down from the stool.

"It was lovely to meet you, Alana." Ben leaned in and kissed my cheek. He looked into my eyes and said, "I hope we meet again." I managed to repeat his words as I looked into his hazel eyes, which appeared to be sparkling, "I hope we meet again, too."

Ben had been the highlight of my day: that first smile outside the church; the second smile inside; eye candy on the dance floor and then, by a happy twist of fate, a nightcap with the man himself.

I floated up the stairs and adjourned to my guest room in the stately home, a little bit drunk and a little bit in love.

Never underestimate the power of a nightcap.

CHAPTER 2

The Morning After

The following morning, I was woken by the phone in my room. It was Jenna. I sat up quickly in an attempt to appear alert and awake, but it was quite clear that I was neither.

"You coming for breakfast, Darling? Ten minutes – meet us in the main dining area."

It was obviously an order. Jenna was still in wedding organiser/bossy bride mode. I needed food, though, to soak up some of those additional wines and the nightcap I had consumed during the last hours of the previous day. Ten minutes?

I had the fastest wash in history, quickly brushed my teeth, grabbed a hair band from my make-up bag, roughly scrunched up my bedraggled sleep-hair into a pony tail, threw on my jeans, my favourite, fading red hoodie and my trainers. I caught a glimpse of myself in the mirror and frowned; surely, I didn't look that bad? But I was too hung-over to care.

I left the room and suddenly remembered where I was. Hoodie and jeans? I was not at the local Travelodge! The corridors of Dorston

Manor were making me feel quite inadequate.

It was only when I was at the bottom of the stairs that I heard his voice and halted in my tracks. Ben the Best Man. There was a roomful of chatter and yet his was the only voice that found a clear frequency in my mind. Why was that?

I walked into the dining room and Jenna instantly swung around to hug me. We'd been friends since our school days but had drifted a bit since the girls had been born.
 "Alana! I hardly saw you yesterday – did you have a good day?"
 "I had a wonderful time and you looked so beautiful, Jenna." She hugged me again and then found another guest to wrap around. Then I was very aware of an odd feeling in the depths of my stomach and some sort of super-human, sixth sense that his gaze was on me. Having not yet got complete control over these new powers, I couldn't work out which part of the room the gaze was coming from, until I got the shock of my life.
 "Good morning", a wonderfully rich voice said into my ear as he walked past to take a seat at the breakfast table.
I could not utter a word but instead smiled and nodded acknowledgement in an attempt to cover up the overwhelming emotion of that moment.

It was hard to say which emotions won out; embarrassment or excitement? Embarrassment had the edge. What was I wearing? The red hoodie was fast becoming my least favourite top ever and I inwardly vowed never to wear it again. Ben was dressed in impeccable black trousers and an expensive-looking blue shirt. He still looked immaculate. How was that fair?

I chose a free seat next to Jenna's mum and opposite Ben. People were exchanging niceties about the hotel, church service etc. I joined in with some polite nods and smiles. Then it happened. He spoke to me across the breakfast table.

"So, Alana, if you are not rushing back, you are welcome to join us back at the house for lunch."

He remembered my name; he actually remembered my name. Our gaze locked across the table and his eyes were quite amazing. They suited him; they were bright, playful, warm and inviting. The disappointing thing was - I did have to rush back; back to my girls Jesse and Amy. They were 4 and 1. I had left them overnight only once before and I needed to be home by lunchtime, as I had promised.

So, I had to decline. Did I detect a disappointment in those bright eyes or was that my hopeful imagination? Breakfast ended and so did the magic. People parted; farewell hugs and pecks on cheeks were everywhere. I hovered around for as long as I could; I didn't really want to leave. I found myself next to Ben Rutherford and I felt a tug on my heartstrings. I liked him a lot.

"It's been great meeting you, Ben", I said truthfully.

"Likewise, Alana; safe journey home." He kissed me on the cheek and I felt his hand on my arm. We smiled at each other and I walked away.

I got into my little Fiesta and drove home in a very odd mood. I was carrying some sort of extra weight. It took me a few weeks to realise that the extra weight was Ben – he had moved into my head, made himself comfortable in the corner of my mind and didn't look as if he was planning to move anytime soon: big issue.

Never underestimate wearing the right clothes at the right time.

CHAPTER 3

The Master Plan

Four weeks after the wedding, I was still reliving the church, the nightcap and the breakfast table. By the fifth week, I was completely fed up with the hopeless, never-ending trail of thought. It was like a film replaying over and over again; then the credits would appear at the end: 'to be continued....'. Yet how could it be continued if I never saw him again? After all, I had never met him before the wedding, so chances were I would never be in the same place at the same time with him ever again. Why was it even going through my head? I had only spent an hour or so with the man plus a brief coffee and croissant moment. Why were those thoughts consuming me? There was only one thing for it – I needed to rebalance; I needed my world to be put back in perspective – I needed Frankie, my best friend, my little sis.

Frankie sat opposite me, grinning cheekily. I finished telling her the whole "Ben" story.

"Alana, I have never ever seen you like this!" She raised her glass and I raised mine and we "ch-chinged" our drinks.

"What are we celebrating?" I was confused!

"You, finding a man you are head over heels about!" Frankie knew me so well. Head over heels just about covered it.

"Yes I found him; but now I've lost him! Literally. I might not ever see him again." Even as I said the words, my heart sank in my own emotional ocean.

"Well, do you know where he lives or where he works?"
It was a good question. I racked my brains for an answer. What had

he told me during the magical nightcap?

"He works in the City; he's got an office at the Royal Court, near Westminster. He's a barrister, soon to be promoted. I think he said he had an apartment near the Strand."

Frankie smiled again, as if we'd won the lottery. Then a very bright 100W light bulb switched on in my head; not an energy-saving bulb that's never quite bright enough - this was a full-on illumination.

"I am going to write to him." Suddenly, the ache in my heart was replaced by a skipped beat. Frankie once again raised her glass and we "ch-chinged" to the master plan. Everything was always better after an evening with Frankie.

Never underestimate the re-balancing power of your best friend.

CHAPTER 4

The Letter

"Dear Ben,

Hello! I hope this letter finds you eventually. It's Alana, Jenna's friend. We met at the wedding last month. You are probably wondering why on earth I am writing to you, so here's the deal...

I really enjoyed the time we spent together at the wedding and I felt a strong connection with you that I think is pretty rare. You have lingered on my mind since then and I just thought it might be nice to meet up sometime for a drink.

I understand completely if you don't want to, or don't even remember who I am but it was great to meet you and I'd love to get to know you better.

Take care,

Alana"

I read the letter back and smiled. It was what I wanted to say. I had found his work address online, put the letter in the local post box and felt very happy with myself. The fact that I had made a move felt so much better than standing in a stagnated thought pond. I texted Frankie:

ALANA – FRANKIE: "Posted! xx"
FRANKIE – ALANA: "Excellent! xx"

It was only when I got back home that the nasty little nagging gremlins appeared from all corners of my head, interrogating me with their questions.
   "What if he doesn't remember who you are?"
   "What if he never gets the letter?"
   "What if he gets the letter and thinks you are a crazy bunny boiler?"
   "What if he doesn't reply?"
It was the last question that stayed with me all evening. "What if he doesn't reply?" I didn't have an answer. How would I feel? I didn't know. I tried to put it to the back of my mind but the thought of that letter sitting in a sorting office somewhere had started to make me feel a little nauseous. The Master Plan suddenly disintegrated before my eyes. "What if he doesn't reply?"

You cannot take it back
You cannot take it back
So lay your head down peacefully
You cannot take it back.

And what will be will be
And what will be will be
So lay your head down peacefully
For what will be will be

Never underestimate the nagging, negative effect of gremlins.

CHAPTER 5

The Deadline

After the initial 21 days of eagerly checking the post for the heart-felt reply, a new kind of doom lingered over my days. Life was challenging raising two children under five but it was a challenge I loved.

We'd been in Reading for a year. Jesse had just started Nursery; it was a relief to mingle with familiar adults every morning and I began to invest in a few 'cup of tea and a chat' friendships from the school. Amy loved socialising and charmed everyone with her cheeky little grin.

I'd bumped into my amazing drama teacher and lifelong friend, Scarlet, a few months before. I'd broken down in tears when hearing myself say, "I don't know what I'm going to do; I've got no job and no prospects but I've got two little angels who depend on me. I can just about afford to feed them." My Mum and Dad would never have seen us go short but it wasn't the point; I was their Mum, their one and only reliable parent, and I was failing them.

"Alana, open your own Drama School. You've got your

qualifications from before Jesse was born. Get some leaflets printed and do it." Scarlet was always so empowering.

"I can't. I didn't do any teaching in Manchester; I don't have the experience; I don't have the energy."

"You have the qualification; that's all you need. What have you got to lose?"

I dismissed the idea at the time but as the months went past, I wondered whether I should take her advice. I filled my days with activities for the girls, while continually training with Scarlet to improve my singing and drama techniques but a cloud hovered above my head, threatening to shower at any point. At times I just wished it would rain, pour down in fact, so that the cloud would disperse and let the sunshine peek through. It was hard to pinpoint which negative emotion was most responsible for the creation of the cloud...anxiety, regret, loneliness, embarrassment, stress, resentment, sadness, as all those emotions touched my heart a lot of the time. Then there was, of course, the daily lack of reply from Ben that added to the disappointment.

One evening, I climbed into bed, with an overwhelming sadness and felt an internal slap on my face. Something inside me snapped. An inner Sergeant Major started shouting in my ear:

"What are you doing?"

I was shocked at first, as it literally felt like a physical smack.

"You are turning into a pathetic mess!"

I was still silent as I knew it was true.

"What are you going to do about it?"

It was a good question but I had taken a dislike to the tone of questioning and I picked up the 'Heat' magazine by my bed to distract from the internal beating. Finally, my kind, internal voice found something to say:

"I will not check the post with hope every day. I will focus on everything else in life. I will keep the door open for Ben Rutherford for 6 months. December 2000; that's the deadline. If I don't hear back, then I will absolutely move on from that fairytale. Six months. Time starts...now.

The Sergeant Major nodded in agreement that it was an acceptable deal.

Never underestimate dark clouds.

CHAPTER 6

Deadline Day - December 2000

Well, it came and it went. December 2000. It had been a long six months. A personal struggle, mostly because I had been living under that annoying cloud of doom which was permanently in my sky. I had begun to get my fighting gloves on, determined to prove to myself that I was a fighter and that I would survive the difficult days but I was rarely convinced.

A year before I met Ben Rutherford, I had left my husband, my marriage and my existence in Manchester. I call it an 'existence' because it was no life. Jesse was 3 and Amy had been a tiny baby, just four weeks old, when I finally had the courage to walk away. It had been an incredibly turbulent four-year relationship. I had made some extremely naive and misguided decisions at the age of 17. In fact, at times I wondered whether, during my 18th year, I had been temporarily deaf, dumb, blind and insane, all at the same time: deaf, because I had heard none of the alarm bells ringing in my ears; dumb, because I should have known that a quick-fire romance with a man of 26 was going to end badly; blind, because I could not see the massive pitfalls right ahead of me, moving up North and starting a new life away from my family and friends, and insane, because none of it made any sense. I had been a sensible girl until that point. The most sensible person I knew. It didn't add up. Temporary insanity was the only answer.

December 2000 was a momentous month in many ways. The darkness that followed my soul around like a bad smell was tainting every part of my life. I was sitting on the sofa one morning and glanced up at my parents' bookshelf. It was a shelf of complete randomness. One book caught my eye...'Life 101: Everything We Wish We Had Learned About Life in School, But Didn't.' The title resonated with my inner core and immediately I thought of all the hard lessons I had learnt over the last five years. Why hadn't they taught me all that at school? Instead, I learnt French verbs that I'd never used and since forgotten.

I browsed through the old, discoloured pages. It was almost too dusty to touch and the pages made me cringe but I looked in the contents and a chapter title leapt out at me:

"WHAT DO YOU WANT?"

I had not read a book for a long time; I was too busy to read. Jesse and Amy always needed me and when they didn't need me, I was too tired. I put the book back on the shelf and got on with my day.

It was later that evening, when I felt the heaviness of life weigh down on my head, that I thought again about that book.

"WHAT DO YOU WANT?"

Almost immediately I answered,
    "I want to be happy"
    "I want to find myself"

Two very powerful statements that made me conclude that I must be sad and lost. It was completely accurate. I wondered what that book had to teach me. What would it tell me that I didn't already know? Surely, it was worth a read. I found myself returning downstairs and took the dusty old book up to bed. I went straight to page 229 –

"What do you want?" I didn't like the type-face but then I was just picky with things like that.
"Would you like a list from one to ten?" Well, I guess that would be good but one to ten? I only had 2 wants: to be happy and to find myself.
"Follow each step and please write your answers down." This was a bit formal, wasn't it? I looked around my little room. No pen. Great. I read on.
"Write down everything you want. Don't worry about attainability or relative importance." Then it hit me. I didn't know what I wanted. I wanted to be happy and to find myself but what would make me happy? And how would I find myself?. What did I want? And then one sneaky, completely out of the blue voice said, "Ben Rutherford".

It crossed my mind that it was December 2000. He had missed the deadline. I had written him a nice letter, perhaps a little forward, but surely it had deserved a reply, even if it was a polite "Thanks for the letter. I think you are completely insane. Have a nice life." But could I be sure the letter had reached him? I'd marked it 'private and confidential' but what if someone else had read it and it had never got to his desk?

I shook my head in dismay. Why was I even thinking about that man 6 months on? Surely, I was once again showing signs of insanity. I resolved to get a pen the next day and complete step one of "What do you want?" I was also determined that I would not be writing Ben Rutherford's name on any want list of mine. He had missed the boat. End of story.

Never underestimate finding the right book at the right time.

CHAPTER 7

The List

(Excerpt from 'Life 101: Everything We Wish We Had Learned About Life in School, But Didn't' by Peter McWilliams)

WHAT DO YOU WANT?

1. Would you like a list from one to ten? Follow each step and please write your answers down. Write down everything you want. Don't worry about attainability or relative importance.

2. Include all things you currently have that you want to maintain.

3. When you feel the list is complete, set it aside and do something else.

4. Return to the list. Did you think of any more wants during the break?

5. Read the list. Cross off any that seem silly or trivial.

6. Classify each want into one of three categories: (A) those that are very, very important to you; (B) those that are very important to you and (C) those that are merely important to you. If a want isn't important enough to make a (C), cross it off.

7. On a clean sheet of paper, copy all your As. If there are ten or more, stop. If there are not yet ten, copy all your Bs. Stop. If there are not yet ten As and Bs, copy all your Cs. Stop.

8. With your new list (the A-B list) choose the one thing on that list you want the most. Write that on a third sheet of paper. Cross that item off the A-B list. Do this nine more times and stop.

9. You should now have ten items written on the third sheet of paper. Look at the list. Number these one through ten. There's your list. This is what you want.

(1) Maintain great relationships with the girls and family
(2) Maintain sistership with Frankie
(3) Run a successful drama school
(4) Take girls on holiday
(5) Have a great relationship with a great man
(6) Read a book
(7) Write a book
(8) Go to a spa
(9) Be happy
(10) Find myself

There – the final list. It had taken many fragmented hours to complete. The hardest part had been getting started. I had for so long been thinking of everyone else's needs that my own had been buried deep underground but, as I sat with the plain page and pen in hand, ever so slowly ideas were crawling up to the surface. One idea led to another, until I had 30 wants. I crossed off a few trivial desires, one being 'a Terry's Chocolate Orange Bar' because I found one in the kitchen cupboard. Instant gratification I think you would call that. Other things crossed off included 'a new pair of shoes', 'no money worries' and 'a new car'. I did actually really want the new pair of shoes. I could replace number (5) with them. After all, I almost wrote, 'have a great relationship with Ben Rutherford' and I had vowed not to put him anywhere near the list. I'd perhaps cheated by rewording it 'great man'. Who was I kidding? I was certainly not fooling my Sergeant Major voice.

"What are you doing?" I quickly crossed off number (5) and replaced it with 'Have a great relationship with a great pair of shoes'. Yes, that was better.

I looked long and hard at the list. My girls were top of it, as they always would be. I studied each number in turn: (2) was a want; (3) was a pipe dream but Scarlet's words kept reverberating around my head. Perhaps I could start up a drama class? (4) was a tough one; (5) a nice idea; (6) an impossibility with no time on my hands. It had been difficult enough to read one single chapter. It would take me a year to read a book; (7) I'd always enjoyed writing at school but who was I trying to fool? I was no author (8) something Frankie and I had talked about; (9) be happy – well, the instructions said attainability wasn't important; (10) find myself – I was going to need a very detailed map for that one but in the last few hours I had let off a flare. Perhaps there was hope.

Never underestimate finding a pen.

CHAPTER 8

The Invitation

"Dear Alana, Jesse and Amy,
We would love you to attend
the Christening of Andrew
at Dorston Church
on Sunday, 9th November 2003
There will be a feast back at the house, where you are all welcome."

I stared at the invitation. Over three years had passed since Jenna and Michael's wedding but suddenly it felt like yesterday. A very strange set of emotions came over me: a brief excitement at the prospect of a big gathering to show off my beautiful girls and then a heavy dread that a certain person might also be there. I could not even mention his name.

Over the past three years, I had given myself a dead arm so many times when I thought about how stupid I'd been to send that ridiculous letter. What had I been thinking?

I looked at the invite again. The chances were that he would not be able to attend anyway. I had heard through the grapevine that he had been promoted and his job was keeping him very busy. How had I heard that? I had met with Jenna soon after Andrew was born and she had been as proud as punch to tell me of her brother-in-law's amazing news.

As I had sat there listening and smiling politely, I was once again chastising myself for being a complete embarrassment. I had sent a letter, a declaration of feelings, to a top, leading Barrister. Brilliant! Only me. I had never mentioned the letter to anyone but Frankie. At least I had some tact.

For the rest of the day, I pondered on possible scenarios if I decided to attend the christening, the worst one being that I turned up at the church and he saw me and started laughing and telling everyone that I was a desperado. How I wished my mind would not run so wild. I got a grip and decided that I was a different person from who I was back then. A little more self-assured, a little more confident, a bit better dressed. Oh, but hang on. I was still driving the same rust-bucket of a car. Perhaps I had not gone up in the world as far as I first thought.

A lot had happened in the last three years. I had been on numerous girls' nights out with Frankie and friends to various London night spots. I'd had several flings with men who were always more interested in me than I was in them. I liked the attention and excitement of a new admirer but as soon as they started to mention feelings, I was off.

I plucked up the courage to start my first drama group in January 2001. It had been slow to establish and I'd contemplated giving it up after a few months of low numbers but Scarlet had insisted that I stuck at it. After a year, I was running 2 groups. After 2 years, I was running 3. I had just decided to do things properly and opened a business bank account under the name 'Alana Drama'. The venture was not making much money but it was giving me a focus and I was thankful for that.

I was starting to enjoy getting up in the mornings and now that the girls' sleeping patterns had matured, I was feeling much more rested. I felt like I was the same girl that I was three years ago, only a little more steady on her feet. Dark clouds still hovered some days but clear skies had started to frequent my days more often.

The girls were growing rapidly and increasingly more special every day. Jesse was now 7 and Amy 4. Both pushed their luck at times but, on the whole, they were amazing girls and I relished the position of mother as I grew into the role. I had celebrated my 25th birthday and was relieved to be getting older numerically. I'd felt 90 some days when I'd first moved to Reading; empty, listless and exhausted with life.

I found myself writing an RSVP to Jenna, accepting the invite. I had a gut feeling he wouldn't be there and seeing Andrew christened would be lovely. Plus, it would be a good excuse to buy a new pair of shoes.

Never underestimate how wrong gut feelings can be.

CHAPTER 9

The Godfather

I pulled up into the church car park and, yes, as I had predicted, my car was still the oldest vehicle by a mile. However, it was not the dirtiest, as I had purposely been to the £2.50 Tesco Value Car Wash to make my little Fiesta as respectable as he could possibly be.

My girls were a bit sleepy from the drive but they soon perked up when they saw Uncle Bob, Jenna's child-friendly father; not a real uncle but rather an adopted one. The girls had bonded with Bob and his wife after a visit to them earlier in the year.
"Girls!" He grabbed both of them, one in each arm, and carried them towards the church, both of them giggling uncontrollably. I gave an inner smile. Nothing beat that feeling of seeing your children happy.

I saw a few friendly faces in the foyer and got chatting with an elderly couple I'd met at the wedding. Jesse had decided where we were going to sit and beckoned me over urgently, as if she was worried a stranger might take my seat. I sat down in between my girls and felt Amy nestle in towards me. She was still tired from the journey and looked a bit unnerved about Jesus on the cross.

I was relieved that there was no sign of the unmentionable man. My theory of his busyness was confirmed. Good.

Jenna and Michael looked very nervous and tired. The other three couples with babies looked almost identical. Parenting was harsh in the first year.

Amy asked, in a whisper, if she could go to the toilet. Damn. I should have made them go before we entered the church. Parenting error No. 2051. I ushered them to the toilet and back again as quickly as was humanly possible. Phew, the service was just beginning. We sat back down in our seats and then...

I saw the back of his head.

A sharp intake of breath involuntarily made me sit up straight. A little Victor Meldrew voice inside groaned "I don't believe it!" He was standing next to Michael. I was distracted by an annoying child who was kicking the pews with his feet. I turned to see the boy more clearly. Surprise, surprise! Well, at least he had grown out of 'Bob the Builder', I suppose.

I watched the service with increasing discomfort as I was very aware that my eyes kept returning to the back of his head, completely involuntarily. I forced myself to look away but within seconds, they were back there, taking a sneaky glance. Fortunately, he had not seen me. It became clear that he was the Godfather. He stood proud, just as he had done in his best man duties. Of course he would be there, he was Andrew's Uncle, after all. How could I have thought otherwise? Once again, I found myself surveying the church and wondering if he had brought a 'plus one' with him. There were a few possible females strewn around but who knew?

Amy started to fidget and sucked her thumb, a sure-fire indication that the service should have ended by then. I stroked her hair and she looked up and smiled. I was brought back to earth.

The christening complete, an announcement was made by Uncle Bob that we were all welcome back to his and Auntie Grace's house for tea and scones. I knew he would be expecting us to go.

It was a little drive from the church. Jesse and Amy skipped to the car and were excited to be going to Uncle Bob's house, as he had a soppy dog who favoured children. Like owner, like dog.

As I parked outside the house, I felt a bolt of nerves hit my stomach. The letter. The shame. The embarrassment. Another dead arm. Before I could think about it anymore, Jesse and Amy were out of the car and running towards the house. As I walked up the drive, I decided to just mingle with everyone else and avoid all contact with him.

I pushed open the door and right there, in the hallway, looking straight at me, was Ben Rutherford. A two-second awkwardness occurred but I looked away, smiled "hello" to a random stranger and side-stepped into the front room. I tried to analyse whether the brief look I saw in his eyes was one which said, "You are the one who sent the letter" or "Who are you?" It wasn't important. What _was_ important was that I avoided him now at all costs.

Never underestimate avoiding some people at all costs.

CHAPTER 10

Déjà vu

The great thing was that the house was full of familiar faces, young and old. I was able to keep mingling whilst successfully avoiding Ben Rutherford. All too regularly I was tuned into that frequency – his well-spoken, delightful voice - but purposely switched off and moved further away, so that my radar would not pick up on his broadcasts.

Until it happened. Auntie Grace called my name.

"Alana dear, will you go and help Bob in the kitchen; he is getting himself all worked up about the tea."
"Of course, I am on my way."
Jesse and Amy were upstairs playing with the numerous children of the family, so I took myself off to the kitchen.

I walked into the room to find Uncle Bob counting china cups...but he was not alone. The Godfather was filling up the kettle at the sink. I almost did an impressive switch turn straight back out but then he saw me."Hello again! We met at the wedding, didn't we?" He put the kettle down and shook my hand. Yes, you read that right.

Firstly, he had to check that we'd met at the wedding. Secondly, he shook my hand. Could this get any worse?

"Yes, that's right. It's Ben, isn't it?" Touché. If he didn't quite remember he had met me, then I wouldn't quite remember his name.

"Yes." At this point he looked straight into my eyes.

"Alana, I need 11 teas. Any chance you could help an old man out?" Uncle Bob put his firm and lovely arm around my shoulder, "I need to check on the guests."

"I'll help", Ben said, as he plugged in the kettle. How could a man possibly look that good plugging in a kettle?

"Congratulations on becoming a Godfather" I said, smiling over at Ben. It was quite obvious that he did not remember me that well and so clearly had not received the letter. The previous three years of dead arms could now cease. This was very good.

"Thank you!" he leaned back against the kitchen top, folded his arms confidently and smiled right into my soul. Oh no, not again!

"Andrew is adorable. I am already training him to like rugby. That is a Godfather's role."

"Rugby? Oh dear", I frowned.

"Not a fan?" he asked. I frowned again disapprovingly and he laughed. "I like my sport but rugby is just organised wrestling with an odd-shaped ball."

Again, he laughed and smiled. 'I must stop looking at him when he smiles because I do not want another three years of this.'

The kettle boiled and he carried it over to my orderly row of cups. As he came closer, I smelt his aftershave. This was a disaster. I would have to exit the kitchen as soon as the teas were made.

"So, how are your two girls?" Ben asked warmly. So, he remembered that fact.

"They are busy playing with the others upstairs. They are doing well, thank you."

At that point, I was very close to asking how his girlfriend was, just to see if he had one but that was so incredibly obvious that I literally bit my tongue.

Ben filled the cups with water as I poured the milk. At one point, our arms touched and I glanced across at him.
   "This is good teamwork", he said, smiling.
   "I agree. This could be a new career path for us."
He laughed again. I was not deliberately trying to be funny but he seemed to have laughed on three occasions in the last three minutes.

The teas were distributed and somehow I found myself entangled in a conversation with Ben about the state of education, the current Formula 1 standings and various other current affairs. It was as if I had been put in a trance. Nobody else in the room appeared visible to me. It lasted a long time. It had been light when we had started talking and now it was pitch black outside. Déjà vu.

After several more topics were covered, including future holiday plans, our joint love of Covent Garden, Uncle Bob's crazy dog and our current job situations, the party was starting to wrap up.
Ben started to collect some cups and I joined in the task. We returned them to the kitchen and for the first time, I felt awkward. We were alone and I heard Ben take a big intake of breath.
   "Alana", he was looking straight at me. I was just about to reply when Jesse and Amy came running in with a party bag. Oh, the excitement of a pink balloon and refreshers necklace was all too much for Jesse. Her eyes were happy and wide.

I saw Ben smile as he dutifully filled the dishwasher and the moment was gone. We parted with a "Lovely to see you again" and I felt his hand on my arm for what seemed like a long time.

It was only during the drive home that my mind began to wonder what he had been about to say in Uncle Bob's kitchen. It had seemed like it could have been the start of a deep and meaningful statement but perhaps that was just my imagination running wild again. He may well have been about to say "Alana, would you like a biscuit?"

The annoying thing was, I would never know. I focused on the road ahead, focused on Radio One and the chart show, focused on checking my girls were OK. However, in the corner of my mind, a spotlight was shining on Ben Rutherford. The little squat he had set up three years ago looked a lot more like a home now.

"Alana..." his voice replayed again and again to me that night as I went to bed and was still going at 3am; a bit like when your neighbours are having a party and all you hear is the repetitive, monotonous thud, thud, thud. Not amusing.

Never underestimate unsaid words.

CHAPTER 11

Cocktails

"Tell me EVERYTHING!" Frankie said excitedly as we sat down on our favourite bar stools. We took a sip of our Cosmos and then I proceeded to tell her 'EVERYTHING'.
She sat there, glued to the story like it was a best-selling audio book, smiling slyly towards the end.

"So...you are telling me he did not excuse himself to go and speak to any other guests for two whole hours?" Frankie waited eagerly for my confirmation.

"Well, no, he didn't. But then neither did I. We just chatted and laughed the entire time." I took a bigger sip of my drink this time.

"He definitely likes you, Alana. Definitely." She smiled again triumphantly. "This is very good!"

"No, it's not good at all!." I exclaimed.

"Why not?" Frankie was confused.

"It's not good news because now I will not see him again unless Jenna and Michael have another child and that will be at least another 9 months and possibly never! I cannot, absolutely will not, be writing another letter and so, that is that."

I surveyed the bar for potential candidates for filling Ben's place in my mind. Unfortunately, there was no-one who caught my eye.

"I see what you mean but I have a feeling you will meet again and when you meet again, you will know that he likes you!" Frankie was doing her best to make me feel better but the harsh reality was that, for the last week, I had been lost in tortured thoughts of unrequited love. I could not bear the thought of another three years of having Ben Rutherford in my head. After seeing him on Sunday, it was like all the colours of a fading picture had been brightened and enhanced back to their original beauty. It was hard to ignore.

"I think we need to talk about you", I said to Frankie, who was looking as stunning as ever. She always managed to look beautiful even when she wasn't trying.

The evening sped past, as it always did when we were together. We had danced our little feet off and continued consuming cocktails. At 2am, we stumbled across the road, arm in arm, laughing at ourselves and feeling enormous pangs of hunger.

"Cheeseburger?" Frankie asked as we approached our regular kebab haunt.

"It is definitely cheeseburger time!"

As we waited in line with all the other drunken people, Frankie turned to me and said, "You've got to write to him again!"

I shook my head defiantly and felt a strength rise up inside me. "Nope, that's it. Dream over. Finito.. End of story. We shall never mention his name again." I felt better, stronger but as soon as I sobered up at 5am, the love came streaming back into my heart. Damn.

Never underestimate internal squatters.

CHAPTER 12

Mystery Man

A few days after my girls' night out with Frankie, I received a text from an unknown number:

"Hey there, we met the other night. I said I would take you for dinner. When are you free?"

I looked at my phone and could not instantly work out who it was from. I put down the 'Daily Mail Sudoku' and thought back to Saturday night. Something was coming back to me; a blurred vision of me giving a man my business card. Why had I thought that was a good idea? But then, after a few Cosmos, everything seemed like a good idea. There was no name on the text to jog my memory further and my mind could not conjure up a detailed mug shot of this man in my head. I decided to see if my partner in crime could remember him more than me:

ALANA – FRANKIE: "Urgent need for witnesses! Who on earth did I give my number to on Saturday? xx"

I reread the text from the mystery man. I had made the assumption it was a man because I had definitely not given my number to any women! It was a good text, short and to the point.

FRANKIE – ALANA: "Oh, yes! Yes you did! Do you remember, it was that guy you were talking to at the bar who said he was impressed by your false Italian accent? He was <u>VERY</u> good looking. You gave him your card and walked away!"

It was like a coin had been slotted into my head and the memory started to play back. Thank goodness for Frankie. I had been flirting with the barman at the time and asked if he had any Pinot Grigio or Semilion Chardonnay and for some reason, I had thought I would sound more appealing if I was Italian. The result was, more realistically, that I sounded incredibly stupid and drunk! Indeed, I had heard this mystery man chuckling at me and I glanced over. He had flashed a very handsome smile my way and said, "I know a wonderful Italian restaurant. You should let me take you one day." I had confidently and smoothly reached into my bag, whipped out my 'Alana Drama' business card and handed it to him.
  "Good idea", I had said as I walked past him and relayed the event to Frankie, who had then high-fived me in her proud sister role! I had not given the man a second thought, probably because, yet again, my mind had been consumed by the multiplying twists of Ben Rutherford. However, there was that mystery man, within the 3-day (he's interested) rule.

I decided to wait a little while before replying so as not to appear too keen, although perhaps I should appear keen. I did fancy a lasagne. Later that day, after many hours of deliberating a reply, I finally sent a text to the mystery man.

ALANA – MYSTERY MAN: "Bonjourno! Thank you for the dinner invitation. I would like to accept. However, I do not know your name."

I didn't reply with a kiss. I did not make a habit of kissing strangers, not whilst sober anyway.
MYSTERY MAN – ALANA: "My name is Antonio."

I laughed out loud. He had to be kidding! He had clearly made up an Italian name but I liked that. Humour was always a good starting point. The Italian banter continued all evening and eventually it got down to the nitty-gritty of arrangements; time, location etc. I was warming to his friendly, ever-so-slightly flirtatious manner and by midnight, he had convinced me that a dinner date with him would be well worth the effort. Let's face it – dates <u>were</u> effort. I would be meeting Antonio in 4 days time. That's if I could get my parents to babysit for a few hours. Fingers crossed.

Never underestimate a welcome distraction.

CHAPTER 13

Timing

Date day arrived and I was in a positive frame of mind. I wore my new fitted jeans and a pretty blue top. I had been in the middle of straightening my hair when my Dad appeared with a pile of post.

"These came this morning for you love, probably all bills!" I gave my Dad a thank you thumbs up and he smiled as he left the room. I threw the post onto my bed and noted that there was a cream envelope beneath the usual, crisp white bills.

I finished my hair, make-up, perfume, slipped on my heels and checked the time. Twenty minutes early, an absolute miracle. I always allowed an hour to drive to London so had time to rummage through the post before I left. I picked up the cream envelope, which intrigued me. It was a hand-written envelop; odd. Then I saw the postmark:

'Westminster'

I stared at the writing and stared at the postmark. I alternated between the two for a few minutes. It couldn't be. It just couldn't be. I felt a paralysis in my hands; I was afraid to move in case the envelope disappeared back into my imagination. Eventually, I tore it open, careful to preserve it as best I could. I took out the quality paper, unfolded the letter and skipped to the very end. Low and behold...

'Ben x'

My stomach flipped a complete 360 turn and I folded the letter back up quickly. I don't know why I did that, as you'd imagine I would have been very eager to see why Ben Rutherford was writing to me but for some reason, I just didn't want to read it. I likened the feeling to having that all-important exam results envelope. Your fate is in it's hands and you have to steady and ready yourself for any, and every, eventuality. I reached for my phone.

ALANA – FRANKIE: "Do not faint. Ben Rutherford has written to me."

I sent the text and within seconds had the reply.

FRANKIE – ALANA: "What???? Massive news. You have to call me! xx"

I texted back to explain that I had to go out but would update her after my date. Which reminded me, I had to get going. I took another look at the envelope and the postmark and tucked it inside my bedside drawer. I was not ready to read it.

I grabbed my coat and kissed my girls goodnight. They were sleepy already and would no doubt be snoozing by the time I was tucking into my starter of garlic bread.

I left the house and the cold, autumnal air caught me off guard. I took a deep breath, realising it was my first conscious one of the day. What had happened to the 7am meditation ritual that had proved to be such a momentous life change in October? Habits formed, habits forgotten. No time to ponder on that now. I shook off the momentary disappointment in myself and started to strut successfully in my heeled boots at a fast pace towards my car.

As I approached it, I realised that all I could see in my head was the hand-written name 'Ben x'

Once in the car, I took a look at myself in the rear view mirror. My eye make-up was a little better than usual, as I had allowed more time in my date preparation schedule. I rummaged around in my CD collection and decided I would choose the 'Happy Songs' CD for a bit of a pre-date boost. I had an hour's drive ahead of me into London but I liked driving; it gave me time to collect my thoughts. I was halfway down the M4 when I realised that collecting my thoughts that day was a really bad idea. All I could think about was Ben's letter, sitting in my top drawer...unread.

Why would Ben Rutherford be writing to me? A tiny little thought seeped into my mind. Was he replying to my letter? From 3 years ago? Had he just received it? Or another possibility was that he was informing me of something Michael and Jenna related; a surprise party or something? That was more plausible.

My pre-date excitement was diminishing fast. In fact, by the time I reached Chiswick, it had practically disappeared. I turned off the 'Happy Songs' because, frankly, they were far too happy for this situation. I knew what I had to do.
I pulled over into a deserted bus lane and reached for my phone.

ALANA – ANTONIO: I am so sorry. Family matters have got in the way. I will not be able to meet you tonight."

I immediately felt worse. It was not something I did often, stand up a date. A decent one as well. But in my mind, reading the letter had become a little bit of an emergency. How could I sit eating lasagne, trying to make conversation, when all the time I would be itching to get back to my bed to reach into that drawer?
It would not have been fair. So at the earliest opportunity, I turned back around and headed home, feeling like a possessed fool. If it had been anybody else's name on that letter, my response would have been calm and collected but it was not 'anybody else', it was Ben Rutherford.

I put my foot on the accelerator.

Never underestimate unread words.

CHAPTER 14

The Letter

"Dear Alana,

I am writing to you because I have a confession. Three years ago you wrote me a lovely letter. At the time, life was complicated with my job and I had recently split with a girlfriend. I kept meaning to write back to at least be polite but I am afraid that I did not follow through with that intention.

I realise it was a brave and bold thing to put your feelings on the line as you did and I am sorry that I left you hanging. I am hoping you will not do the same to me as revenge?

I, like you, enjoyed your company equally and, having seen you again, wondered whether you would like to meet up for dinner one evening. I could travel to you as there is a direct train from London.

It would be good to get to know you better.

Ben x"

I read it once and then I read it again. I studied his handwriting; the ever-so-slightly-slanted ascenders, the joined-up, free-flowing sections. I did not think it possible to fall in love with handwriting but I did.

It fast became a precious gem to me, that letter. I folded it and put it back in the envelope. No sooner had I done it, I missed the words and so opened it up again, re-read it a few times and finally, after the zillionth read, I heard that Sergeant major voice:
"What are you doing?" Obsession was not a word I wanted to be associated with. I must get back in control.

I turned off the light and laid my head on the pillow. I took a deep breath, my second of the day. This breath felt very different. I was breathing in new knowledge. Ben Rutherford had written me a lovely letter. He had missed the deadline by almost 3 years but somehow, that seemed completely insignificant. He had apologised for that. Apology accepted. I was not imagining that there was 'something' there because now I knew he felt it too.

Never underestimate the power of a letter.

CHAPTER 15

The Text

The next couple of days, I floated around in some kind of pink, fluffy bubble. The previous few years of struggles seemed to have vanished in an instant and there I was with the key to the door of a new, brighter future.

I evaluated my feelings and the most wonderful thing was that I had not imagined it. It had been special. I knew it, and had believed it for so long but when the letter never arrived, I started to doubt my sanity (not for the first time). Now, I felt vindicated. I had been telling the truth to myself all those years. I could stop putting myself on trial now.

It was a two-way feeling, as I had suspected when we talked. The way his eyes followed me, the way he held conversation with me, the way he laughed at my little quips. The signs had all been there and I had read them correctly.

A secret smugness surrounded me in everything I did that weekend. As I walked around Tesco's, I observed happy couples choosing their meal for the night and pictured Ben and me doing the same. I let myself daydream about our first kiss, lingering on that thought for slightly too long.

Forty-eight hours after receiving the letter, I decided to text him:

ALANA – BEN: "I am not revengeful and so I have not made you wait 3 years for a reply (although tempting!). Thank you for the letter (better late than never!). It would be lovely to meet with you. Let me know when and where x"

I deliberated over the kiss but felt it was acceptable as he had placed a single kiss after his name on the letter. I knew this because I had engraved that kiss on my forehead. I sent the text. I re-read it a few times, imagining that I was Ben receiving it. Would it make me smile? Yes, I think so.

It was a few hours later when I got the reply:

BEN – ALANA: "Great. Will email you."

No kiss. It was the first thing I noticed and it slightly drained the pink fluffiness from my bubble. Ever so slightly. It made me frown and check my position. The letter was not a marriage proposal. It was not even a girlfriend request. It was simply an invite to get to know each other better. My imagination had set off at full pace, with a jet pack, flying uncontrollably into an unknown space. Time to switch off the engine and return to earth. No kiss.

I went to bed wishing I had not put that single kiss on my text. If I had left it kiss-less, I would have felt I had the upper hand, or at least some sort of control. Equal terms. At that moment, it felt like I had made an error. It would be the first of many.

Never underestimate the amount of hours you can waste over-analysing messages.

CHAPTER 16

The Email

"Re Rendezvous

Dear Alana,

I am so glad you were gracious enough to not make me wait three years. I am sorry again for the very long wait.

Things are very busy work-wise this week but I have a couple of days off next week. How about I travel to Reading and we could go for a bite to eat?

Looking forward to it,

Ben x"

I smiled a big smile. The kiss was back. What had I been worried about? I scolded myself for having wasted a good few hours of my life internally debating the lack of a kiss on the text, which had probably been sent in a hurry.

The email was good. I liked the title. 'Rendezvous'. I emailed back immediately. I was not going to play all those silly games of waiting hours to reply, so as not to appear too keen. I caught myself fleetingly thinking about Antonio, the date I stood up. I had not heard from him since that day and I had felt too guilty to contact him. It was a stalemate. A sad one, though. He had potential. I put the question to myself: "If you were given the opportunity to go out on a lovely date, would you prefer to go with Ben or Antonio?" No sooner had the question finished, the answer was locked in: "Ben".

It took a few emails to and fro to finalise arrangements. Eventually, the date was set – the following Wednesday at a restaurant in town.. It did not take long for me to descend into wardrobe panic. What on earth should I wear? If I tried too hard, it would show; if I didn't try hard enough, it would show. Finding a balance would be my biggest challenge. I had exactly seven days to conjure up the perfect outfit.

ALANA – FRANKIE:"Help! Date with Ben on Wednesday! What am I going to wear?"

FRANKIE – ALANA:"You will be irresistible whatever you wear."

And that's why I loved Frankie.

Never underestimate a wardrobe crisis.

CHAPTER 17

A Perfect Evening

I found myself rushing into town. Typically, my pre-date routine did not go to plan and now I felt flustered and, to be honest, a little nauseous. Deep down, though, in the depths of my soul, there was an excitement I had never felt before.

I was due to meet Ben by the entrance of the car park and I could see his silhouette from across the bridge. My heart skipped briefly and I took a deep breath to steady myself. Then he clocked me and smiled. As we met, he gave me a peck on the cheek and there it was again. That gorgeous aftershave that acted like some sort of magic smelling salt, waking me up from a sleepy coma and making me feel very alive. He looked immaculate once again and I pinched myself inwardly to check this was actually happening.

The evening was everything I had hoped for and more. We talked non-stop about life, work, family, friends, cars, France, sport, food and we smiled, laughed and subtly flirted.

I was aware of an amazing contentment washing over me, as if that was where I belonged, in that very moment. That was who I was, truly, and being with Ben brought out the very best in me, the very happiest me there was.

As we sipped our coffee after a delicious three-course meal, I noticed we were the only people left in the restaurant. Where had everyone gone? It did not matter. Ben had been the only person in the room for the entire three hours. Tom Cruise, Brad Pitt and George Clooney could have walked past our table for all I knew. I wouldn't have noticed. I had been transfixed, captivated and totally at one with the man opposite me.

Then the first silence of the evening fell on us. I looked into my coffee and did not look up until he said "I am so glad you wrote to me all those years ago." I looked up and involuntarily my hand hit my head; a learned behaviour whenever I thought about 'that' letter.

"I wish I had never sent it!" I said, honestly, thinking about the three years of internal torture that followed.

"But, we may not be sitting here now if you hadn't", he smiled brightly across at me. "I've had a lovely evening, with great food and fantastic company." He leaned back into his chair and sipped his coffee, still looking at me.

It was those moments, those little things he did, like leaning back into his chair, that stirred something inside me that made me want to kiss him. Instead, I smiled and said, "Well, when you put it like that, perhaps it was one of my better moves."

He laughed and conversation flowed freely again until we reached his car. I had been in this end-of-date situation before with other men. That awkward moment when you do not know if there will be a kiss on the lips, or a peck on the cheek, or if things had gone really badly, a little wave goodbye, or twist of your heels to run for your life. All had happened to me on previous occasions.

So we stood by his car and we warmly thanked each other for a wonderful evening – it had been wonderful – and then he kissed me, briefly but somehow tenderly, on the lips.

"I'll call you", he said. Then he got into his car, smiled through the window and drove off into the night, while I floated home, on a cloud engraved with the words Ben 4 Alana.

It was the perfect night.

Never underestimate that floating feeling.

CHAPTER 18

And so...

And so, with the perfect night behind me, I had every right to be smiling for days but after the second day, there was no call. The third day came and went in a silent, descending doom. The fourth day, deflation.

I removed the battery from my phone and re-inserted it, just in case some strange Nokia malfunction had stopped calls getting through but I knew this was a pointless exercise.

Frankie had called every day. The worst thing was that I didn't understand. It didn't add up. He had said himself it was a wonderful evening. He had been as happy as me. He had said he would call. Life carried on, as it always did, but my heart, which had been jumping for joy last week, was now slumped in the corner, feeling confused.

> "In the blink of an eye
> Hearts sink
> Never to be rescued, recovered or found
> Left to rust and run aground
> Or so it seems, or is it so?
> Be damned if I will ever know"

I did not understand. The silence did not match the behaviour from the date. Maybe something had happened? This was a viable line of enquiry. I decided to put myself out of my misery:

ALANA – BEN: "Great to see you the other night. How's your week going x?"

I sent it and then got consumed in motherhood, making play dough outfits for a play dough model Amy was making. After several hours, I checked my phone. Nothing.

A slight pain entered my soul. It was hard to establish where the physical pain of the soul is felt, but I felt it. The old saying 'it cuts like a knife" I could vouch for that.

When the girls were tucked up in bed, sound asleep in their beautiful way, I crept into bed and I could think of nothing else. Where was he now? What was he thinking? Surely, if he liked me he would not wait 5 days to call or contact? This went way past the 3-day rule of first meeting. I had never heard of waiting 5 days after a date and no reply from the text seemed to secure my worst fears. Once again, I was back in the dock.
   "Alana, you stand accused of believing Ben Rutherford feels the same way as you, when there is clear evidence to the contrary. How do you plead, guilty or not guilty?"
   "Guilty, with a capital G."
I looked in the mirror. The engraved kiss from the letter had been replaced by a very feint M U G stamped across my forehead. I cleansed, toned and moisturised but it was still there: M U G.

Never underestimate the hurt of deflation.

CHAPTER 19

Why?

Would you believe it, the silence went on, and on, and on? It was like the elephant in the room for me for weeks. Christmas came and went. People would ask me how I was, how my day was going and I would answer cheerfully, "good thanks". On occasions, I even convinced myself but there was a heavy-heartedness, utter confusion and disappointment, which weighed me down persistently. An inner turmoil. I did not even convey to Frankie how deeply it had cut me. She had been lovely, saying all the things that would normally have made me feel better.

"He must be clinically insane if he hasn't called you; well, if he is treating you like this, he is not good enough for you anyway; plenty more fish in the sea." On the surface, these things made sense to me and were all true, but deep down, I just didn't understand.

I let the memory of that evening replay in my mind. Surely, I had not been imagining the amazing chemistry between us; the easy contentedness of our conversation, the looks, the laughs, the sparks? I needed to know for my own sanity.

I took out a notelet from my bedside drawer and started to write:
"Dear Ben,

I really enjoyed our evening together, and was under the impression you did, too. Your lack of communication since has made me think otherwise.

It would be helpful if you could let me know either way as I am starting to feel like a fool. I understand if you do not want to see me again but honesty is always the best policy.

Alana"

I angrily stuck a stamp on it, hunted for his work address and put it on the floor, ready to post in the morning.

It annoyed me that it had gone this far. It annoyed me that I cared so much about the silence. It annoyed me that I'd had no reply to the text. It annoyed me that I had replied to his letter in the first place. Why did he write to me? Why did he get my hopes up, right up to the clouds? It annoyed me that I was free-falling at such a pace down to earth with no parachute. It annoyed me that I appeared to love this man who was clearly difficult. It annoyed me, but mostly it hurt.

Never underestimate the sadness inside.

CHAPTER 20

Not Suitable

Three long, drawn-out weeks later, a cream coloured envelope fell through the letterbox. I picked it up and took it to my room. I had a quiet moment to myself so I opened it with a mix of dread and anticipation.

I glazed over the page. The handwriting. Once again it made me ridiculously weak. I steadied myself and read the words.

"Dearest Alana,

Yet again I find myself apologising to you. I am sorry for any confusion I have caused. I have been confused myself.

I did enjoy our evening together very much. Too much, perhaps. I have done a considerable amount of thinking and I feel that it would be unsuitable to have a relationship with you and I do not feel that I can take on somebody else's children.

You are right that honesty is the best policy. None of this is coming out the way I want it to but I will not re-write it, as I know it's what needs to be said.

I hope we can still be friends. Please call me when you get this, so I can explain more.

Ben x"

There it was. Such beautiful handwriting conveying such a heartbreaking message. A stark, honest message. I had asked for honesty but at that moment, I could think of nothing worse. My two girls were a hurdle he could not jump over to be with me. My beautiful, warm and loving children. It was a rejection of great magnitude. Tears welled in my eyes involuntarily and my head dipped. I shut my eyes to ward off the tears and took a deep breath.

I quickly shoved the letter back into the envelope and into my top drawer. Why were his words so painful to hear? With a torturous need, I read it again, and got stuck re-reading one sentence, "I feel that it would be unsuitable to have a relationship with you." 'Unsuitable'. What did that mean? I felt worse for re-reading it; I felt miserable and despondent. 'Unsuitable'. That was an Oxford University term. 'Unsuitable'. I looked up the definition just to be clear.

<u>Unsuitable:</u>   not fitting or appropriate.

<u>Synonyms:</u>   inappropriate, ill-suited, incompatible

Then it hit me in the face like a tonne of bricks; the truth. <u>I</u> was unsuitable. I was a divorced, single mother of two at the age of 21, living with my parents, with a mediocre education in a state school and who taught part-time drama classes to try to scrape enough money for the week. I drove a rusty Fiesta and watched 'Eastenders'. How did that compare to the son of one of the most respected judges in England, who was educated privately, followed by Oxford University; someone who had property in 2 countries, drove a new, expensive Mercedes and watched 'Antiques Roadshow'.

On paper, it was clear. I was unsuitable. I could not argue. I was Division 2, possibly Vauxhall Conference League and he was top of the Premier League. If the two teams played together, the spectators would laugh at the chances of the underdog. I was the underdog. That's how he saw me. After the 10th reading of the letter, it was how I saw myself. It was a dark day.

Never underestimate honesty.

CHAPTER 21

The Notebook

I spent the next day wallowing in my own Jane Eyre-style pity. I wrote poems of anguish and stared endlessly at the heartbreaking letter. In between, I played with Barbie Dolls, cuddled up watching 'Toy Story' and cooked fish fingers and chips. The everyday went on.

After 24 hours, I was completely fed up with myself and the pattern of thought. When I went to bed, I took out a notebook I had bought for work and never used. I grabbed a pen and began to write and write and write. I wrote a list of emotions I was feeling;

embarrassment
disappointment
hurt
sadness
confusion

and then came an overwhelming bubbling of an emotion I rarely felt: ANGER. I wrote pages of angst-ridden rant about why Ben Rutherford thought he was better than me and, if he had thought that, why had he bothered to write to me in the first place? He knew

I had two children; why would he then use that to put a barrier on what he felt. To be honest, I was much happier in this vexed mood; it seemed more empowering than the pure sadness and disappointment I had been feeling. I re-read the letter from an angry viewpoint and it was like fuelling a fire. 'Unsuitable', pah! The smoke bellowed from my ears. I wrote one last paragraph in my notebook that day:

"Ben Rutherford,

You have had an amazing education, you sometimes come out with words I've never heard of, you own property and a very nice car, you've got a prestigious job and here's me, Alana...I have none of these things...but I know we've got a connection far deeper than status and material things. The one thing I do possess is a very big heart and so I am stating that you are indeed 'unsuitable' for me. Talk to the hand. Bad luck, sunshine. Over and out."

I smiled to myself and slammed the notebook shut. There.

Like the wind, strong against my cheek
You came without a warning
The hope, the dream, flew from my hands
A new day now is dawning
I cannot chase a hopeless case
A kite without a string
I let it go, I turn my back
My eyes let out a sting
Let the rain fall free to cleanse me
Let the night fall on this day
Let me wake up new tomorrow
With no love to wash away

Never underestimate the therapeutic power of having a rant.

CHAPTER 22

Cosmopolitans

So it came to be that the notebook I had ranted in became my best friend that year. I wrote at night when the girls were asleep and, with each page of writing, came a deeper understanding of who I was and how I felt and where my mind wandered to. It astounded me how many pages the words 'Ben Rutherford' appeared in. The anger subsided after a few weeks and an emptiness replaced it. Confusion was also high up on the emotional agenda.

I was bemused as to why he was so prominent in my thoughts. It was not as if we had been married or had a serious relationship, where memories came flooding back to haunt us. There was no basis or reasoning behind the overwhelming sense of attachment I felt for him.

I never did call him so he could "explain more". I thought about it, as you can imagine, many times. I wondered what he would say but I knew, all too well, it would not be anything I wanted to hear. So, that was that. Until...

It was late August and Frankie had invited me down for cocktails and a summer catch-up. We were both in good spirits, feeling positive about work and life in general. She had recently been promoted and my drama school was doing well, so we 'ch-chinged' our glasses 'to our success'. Numerous Cosmos later, Frankie's friend Jodie appeared and they both went up to the bar for our refills. As I sat people-watching, I checked my phone and saw the date...19th August. I turned my phone over so I couldn't see it but it was too late. The thought was there and attached to the thought was an instant flutter of my stomach, which led to a knee-jerk gut reaction to pick up my phone and press 'Compose Text Message'.

I froze in that position until the girls returned.

"What's up?" Frankie clocked my change of mood.
"It's Ben Rutherford's birthday", I said blankly, not really knowing what I was feeling. Frankie instantly understood and looked at the phone in my hand.
"Have you messaged him?" Her eyebrows raised inquisitively but with a softness I knew well.
"No, I stopped myself." I thought this should have sounded more positive than it did. In fact, it sounded downright feeble. "Anyway, let's change the subject!" And we did. However, for the rest of the evening, I was slightly distracted with my own thoughts. A foot in reality and a foot in that world where I often found myself wandering. A world with Ben Rutherford floating around my head. I wondered what he had done for his birthday, who he'd spent it with, was he happy? Then my own personal interrogation began. 'Why didn't you call to let him explain; why did you let contact stop altogether; why are you even thinking about him on his birthday?' It was clever how I could have these internal debates and yet still appear so normal on the outside.

I glanced at the clock above the bar. It was 11.40pm. I told Frankie

I was off to the little girls' room. I picked up my phone and slid it into my pocket.

What I did next cannot easily be explained. It was like cupid was dragging me into it. I was under duress. I pulled out my phone and, for the second time that evening, pressed…'Compose Text Message'. I typed:

ALANA - BEN: "Happy Birthday Ben. Hope you've had a great day. Alana."

Before I knew it, Cupid held his bow to my head and ordered me to press 'Send'. Who was I kidding? I did it all from my own free will. The only consolation to me was that I was sitting on the toilet at the time. It could hardly be called a romantic gesture.

Why, oh why, did I press 'Send'? In that moment, I lost control of the situation and once again would be waiting; waiting for a reply; waiting for a sign that he felt the same; waiting, waiting, waiting. My last question to myself was "Why are you so good at remembering birthdays?" Annoying.

Never underestimate Cupid's arrow.

CHAPTER 23

3.05am

We got back to Frankie's after midnight and both of us were out like a light. One too many Cosmopolitans may or may not have been the cause.

I stirred during the night and checked my phone to see what ungodly hour it was. My head hurt. I squinted to see 3.05am. One new message. Ben Rutherford. Holy Smoke!

My eyes popped wide open as I stared long and hard at the screen. There was no denying that total flip of my stomach. I hadn't felt that since seeing the handwriting on that dreaded letter. The suspense was killing me.

BEN – ALANA: "Alana. What a lovely surprise! So kind of you to remember my birthday and even kinder to text. I've had a great day and you just made it brilliant. Hope all is well with you? Ben x"

I read it with a sigh of relief. Relief that I hadn't had to wait after all. It had been the right thing to do. I had thought of him, let him know, and he appreciated the thought.

Frankie slept soundly in her bed, unaware of the excitement I was experiencing; unaware also that I had sent the birthday text. I would have to tell her in the morning. It was a significant development. Or was it? I lay awake, feeling a sense of déjà vu. All those hopeful feelings flooding back. Was it a sign that Ben Rutherford felt the same? I had transformed his day from great to brilliant. Surely that was an encouraging statement and the speed of reply was impressive.

Before I knew it, the birds were starting to tweet annoyingly outside and the sun peeped in through the trendy blinds. I had not slept a wink since 3.05am. I shook my head in dismay. Why had I wasted yet another night's sleep over Mr Rutherford? Why did I let myself get carried away? The text was not a sign. It was just one polite text in reply to another. No more and no less. In fact, it was not even worth talking about. Not even worth mentioning. I read it one more time, absorbing the warmth of the words and then I deleted it.

Deleted from my phone, yes; deleted from my mind, unfortunately not.

> *"There is only you who reoccurs*
> *So what am I to do?*
> *No matter who or what or why*
> *It all comes back to you"*

Never underestimate recurring thoughts at 3.05am.

CHAPTER 24

To Reply or Not to Reply: That is the Question

The following few days were strange. I was busy with work and the girls but a distant thought was sailing on the horizon. I could not quite remember the wording of Ben's text and I berated myself for impulse deleting. The thing that stuck in my mind was that all important "?" after he said "Hope all is well with you?". If there had been a simple full stop, things would have been easier. Full stop. End of conversation. Done. A question mark, however, seemed to imply that it needed a response and yet, it was not a clear question either. Had the wording been, "How are things with you?" that would require an answer, as it was an obvious question. It rolled around my head for many hours. Should I reply? I stacked up plenty of evidence to support the case that I shouldn't.

    The man hurt you.
    The man is complex.
    The man does not want to raise your children.
    The man didn't remember your birthday.
    The man cannot ask questions.

And only one argument for replying:
    I wanted to.

I looked at both lists in my notebook and wondered if there was anyone else on the planet as ridiculous as me for analysing a question mark on a deleted text from a man I'd only seen 3 times in my life. I doubted it.

I wanted so much to override the evidence and to send Ben a rambling message, telling him all about how things were with me and to ask him a question back, to keep that conversational ball rolling for the rest of our lives, but the thought that he might not then reply to me was one that hit me where it hurt. So, I let the desire to text him gently fade away.

I distracted myself with work and ploughed my passion into it on a daily basis. I eventually confessed to Frankie that I'd sent Ben the birthday text and she backed up my decision to leave it there. She still hadn't forgiven him for having led me on with the letter and the date. She still referred to him as a 'stupid man' for not realising what a catch I was. Frankie once sent me a picture which said:

"If you mess with the Big Sister, then there is always a younger, crazier sister behind her that you don't want to mess with."

This was so true. Frankie was like her star sign, Leo – beautiful, creative, loyal and true, but if you got on the wrong side of her – well – you were never seen again!

Never underestimate how hard it is to resist that 'crazy-in-love' voice.

CHAPTER 25

September Sun

September was a beautiful month. The weather had been particularly kind to England during the summer and continued that way in the early autumn months.

One Saturday evening, Frankie and I decided to meet up with our other girlfriends to make a night of it down by the Thames. We arrived at the pub in plenty of time to have a 'sisters' catch-up before the other arrived.

"So, how are you feeling now about Ben?" Frankie enquired as she poured our first glass of Pinot.
"I'm fine now. It's time to put it behind me. No dreaming and definitely no texting! I'll have forgotten his birthday by next year!"
"Yes. Well, maybe you will find another man who catches your eye tonight!" It was a possibility, as I was feeling good. My hair was freshly cut and coloured; I'd had my eyebrows shaped and tinted and I was wearing a new figure-hugging outfit I'd treated myself to on my shoestring budget. More importantly, I felt good on the inside, perhaps even a little adventurous. My eyes were wide open and ready for a good night.

The other girls arrived and it wasn't long before we were all exchanging stories and updates. We laughed and smiled and consumed various alcoholic beverages, until we heard the DJ setting up. We all smiled, put our glasses down and headed to the dance floor. There was something special about getting all the girls together. We sparked off one another, like a crazy science experiment. Put us all in one room and what did you get? An explosion of confident women, all bouncing ideas off each other, bigging each other up to new heights, boosting us as individuals but somehow, more importantly than that, boosting our team. We were like a tribe. That feeling of connectedness to other humans was hard to match and often we'd forget how important it was until we were all under the same roof again.

That night, we were raising the roof. We strutted and danced our way into the hearts of the bar staff, the DJ and seemed to make friends with almost everyone.

It was in that positive moment that I headed over to the bar and accidentally bumped into a very handsome, bleach-blonde haired man.

"I'm sorry", he said, with an enormous grin which lit up his entire face. I detected an accent.

"Hello", I said, with an equally big grin on my face, produced involuntarily!

"You are by far the friendliest person in this place. What's your name?"

"I'm Alana." I shook his hand to just confirm I was, indeed, the friendliest person in the room, "and you are?"

"I'm Kyle", he said, still smiling straight into my eyes. "Please don't leave without giving me your number."

Wow, that was straight to the point! I nodded for some reason and then found myself skipping towards the bar to complete my mission to get another bottle of Pinot. I turned around to search for my new-found friend Kyle but he was nowhere to be seen.

I returned to the girls, who had sat down for a rest when a dodgy tune was playing.

"Oh my God!" I said, with an excited squeal.

"What?" The girls all knew there was gossip coming.

"I have just met the most handsome man over there and he wants my number!"

Frankie smiled at me and said, "Go and find him and give it to him. What have you got to lose?"

So I did!

Never underestimate being the friendliest person in the room.

CHAPTER 26

Whirlwind

I had often heard the phrase 'whirlwind romance' and thought how wonderful it sounded. Something so powerful it swept you off your feet. I had never really thought of it as a negative thing until I was in the aftermath of a whirlwind romance of my own, which I best describe as a disastrous mess.

Kyle very quickly became entangled in my life after that first night. We'd met up the next day and were both besotted with each other. I was amazed at how we spent so long happily staring into each other's eyes. Kyle was from New Zealand on a temporary visa and was due to go back at Christmas. Neither of us thought too much about that at first; the whirlwind was too much fun. He persuaded me to introduce him to my girls within a few weeks and they warmed to him equally as quickly as I did. My parents didn't mind him staying over and by November, he was becoming part of the furniture.
We had a discussion one night about the possibility of Kyle trying to extend his visa and the thought was a happy one. In fact, my heart was upbeat with the thought of this new future which had sprung itself on me out of the blue.

Then, the thunderbolt struck. I'd started to volunteer as a classroom assistant at the girls' school in September and had been invited along for a meal and drinks with some of the staff, to celebrate a colleague's birthday. It wasn't a partners' thing so Kyle headed to London to meet with his friends. All seemed well until I received a text, halfway through the evening, which had a very strange tone:

KYLE – ALANA: "Who are you with?"

I replied nicely,

ALANA - KYLE: "I'm with the teachers, remember, for Nigel's birthday. How's London xx?"

KYLE - ALANA: "Who are you sitting next to? I see you haven't had time to text me all evening."

I looked at my phone and felt puzzled. Had someone got hold of Kyle's phone? It certainly didn't sound like him?

I looked to either side of me and realised I was sitting next to Nigel and, on the other side, was Dylan, a lively and extremely funny man whom I'd always got on well with.

I sat for a moment and felt acutely uncomfortable with the situation. I didn't like the tone of Kyle's message and I wondered whether it was just my imagination. I texted back the truth:

ALANA - KYLE: "There are loads of us here. I'm sitting next to Nigel and Dylan and Jenny is opposite and it's nice to see them all."

Then there was nothing. No reply for the rest of the evening. I was eating my meal, smiling and nodding but inside, I knew something was wrong. I knew there was a storm brewing. The questions had been cold and direct. What's more, I was an expert in spotting that kind of behaviour. I had been married to a manipulative, controlling man.

The next day, Kyle returned from London as if nothing had happened. He greeted me with a passionate kiss but my kiss was not as responsive. I was holding onto the emotions of the previous day when I'd heard that shrill alarm bell ringing in my ear; possessive, possessive, possessive, possessive. It went on and on. I couldn't ignore it and so I approached the subject later that night.

I will not bore you with the whole conversation. It took a while to get to the nitty-gritty and it was an extremely uncomfortable, deep and meaningful. I will skip to the main headline.

"Alana, I do have to tell you something. I have a Paranoid Personality Disorder."

I stared, stunned and confused. There was a name for a controlling, manipulative person? Kyle then went on to describe his many failed relationships and with each story, I felt more and more anxious that I was sitting in the same room as him; that I was even in the same country as him.

My own memories of having been controlled and manipulated were flooding back; emotions rising up from a grave within, where I thought they'd been buried forever. As I looked into Kyle's eyes, the same eyes that a day ago I'd happily smiled into, I felt cold. I could hear his words entering my head but my mind was elsewhere. Paranoid Personality Disorder – what did that mean? It sounded a little bit dangerous. I suddenly realised that I was scared. Kyle detected the change in my body language; my smile was gone and I was hugging my knees and breathing deeply, to try and get a hold of myself. I searched my soul for something truthful to say to him as he held both my hands in his and told me he loved me. His eyes were now as sad as mine; perhaps he read my mind before the words left my mouth.

"I'm so sorry, Kyle, you have to leave. I cannot be the woman to help you through this. I cannot be the girl to understand. It would break me. I've been broken before and I've only just glued myself back together. Please promise me you will get professional help otherwise this will just happen again and again."

Tears were shed, pleas were made; he made me feel like the Wicked Witch of the West. I was giving up on him so early. It was true, I was. I felt cold and heartless, maybe I was a witch? He packed his bags, crying endless tears. I watched in pain. Then he was gone. Never to be seen again; my happy ending walked out of the door. As I shut it behind him, I realised that the glue I'd used to put myself back together must have been sub-standard because, in that moment, I felt totally shattered; shattered into tiny pieces, yet again; the after-effects of a whirlwind.

Never underestimate the devastating effect of a whirlwind.

CHAPTER 27

The Aftermath

It was not long before word got out about my disaster and aid, in the form of support and kind words arrived via emails and texts from all corners of my world. I had been so excited about meeting Kyle that I'd told practically everyone in my address book. Life mistake No. 2057. It meant that every time I bumped into someone I knew, I would have the same, difficult conversation.

"Hi, Alana, how's the new man?"
"It didn't work, out."
"Oh, I'm so sorry, what happened?"
"He wasn't as right for me as I thought."

My closest friends knew the whole story but I was reluctant to explain the situation too often because every time I did, I felt a little worse and a little more guilty for 'giving up on him so quickly'. Those words rang in my head like an annoying wind chime. When a thought breezed through my mind, there it would be, 'You gave up'.

The hardest explanation I had to make was to the girls, Jesse and

Amy. They asked where Kyle was the morning after he left and I had to explain in the simplest of terms that we wouldn't be seeing him anymore. They looked so sad and Jesse's repetitive "why?" question beat me down to a pulp. In the end, I said, "He just wasn't right for us".

Frankie and the ladies were the ones to save me from myself. I was at a low point when I met with them a few weeks after the event.

"Alana, you absolutely did the right thing. You can't spend your time feeling sorry for the man. Your life would have been hell with him; someone always looking over your shoulder, checking up on you. You would have to justify every phone call. I've been there and done that, honey. You are well rid!"
I loved Natalia's straight talking and I was relieved to feel a little better after hearing her words.

"You've got the girls to think about, too. If you'd let him stay, it would have been worse for them in the long run", Malia chipped in.

"Well you had a bit of fun for a couple of months, anyway", Frankie said, smiling. It was true. It had been fun right up until that last day. It had taught me that I could still open up my heart. It had been broken again but sitting there at the table with my friends, I knew I'd be OK. I knew I'd survive. A little while later, 'Sisters are doing it for themselves' started playing and Frankie caught my eye and smiled. It was our trigger song to burn up the dance floor. That night, my ladies took me from low to medium to high on the happiness scale. I loved them. We loved each other. Sisters doing it for themselves.

Never underestimate letting your friends save you.

CHAPTER 28

The Invite

When I returned from London the following morning, there was an envelope on my desk. I recognised the writing; it was Jenna's. I opened it up and there was an invite to Lilliana's christening in February. I had half been expecting it ever since she'd been born but it still managed to catch me off guard.

My thoughts instantly turned to Ben. He would no doubt be there. The situation seemed worse than last time; the embarrassment would be more acute. Not only would I have to avoid him but I would also have to go in disguise. I couldn't possibly speak to him. Yet, there was a part of me that wanted to speak to him more than anything else in the world; a craving to be in his company and to feel that amazing aliveness and completeness I experienced whenever I was with him. Surely, by now, he would have met a 'suitable' girlfriend, someone from a 'suitable' family, with a 'suitable' education, a 'suitable' job and a 'suitable' car.

I was a little shocked at the bitterness of my thoughts. I wondered whether I should decline the invite. It would probably be the safest and most sensible option, so as not to dig up those emotions again. Out of sight and out of mind.

I knew, however, that I hardly ever took the sensible route. I looked in the mirror and decided that I would go to the christening and not only would I go, but I would show Ben Rutherford that he'd made a big mistake; the biggest mistake of his life, in fact. I had two months to prepare.

Never underestimate that "I'll show you" thought pattern.

CHAPTER 29

The Godfather Part 2

It was a crisp, cold, sunny morning. The girls climbed out of the car and raced across the car park to see Uncle Bob. There was a touch of the déjà vu's about the situation.

I couldn't believe that my Fiesta had lasted five years. It did look a sorry state now; rust overtaking the paintwork like a disease and the engine sounded more like a tractor chugging along than a classic Ford but I did not feel inadequate at all. I patted 'Sylvester' on the bonnet and was grateful that he had got us to the church safe and sound. I strolled with confidence across the gravel that I had once been so tentative over. My hair swished around my shoulders and I felt in charge of my emotions. I was pleased to be feeling that good.

As I entered the familiar church, I saw him straight away. He was talking with Michael and smiling in a warm, genuine way. I remembered that smile and my heart fluttered slightly. I averted my gaze to Uncle Bob, who was gesturing to me to come and sit by him and the girls.

I smiled and chatted to Jesse and Amy. They were taking everything in, asking questions and grinning broadly at Uncle Bob. I glanced Ben's way for a millisecond and looked away instantly, as he was looking straight at me. I vowed not to look again.

The ceremony predictably lasted for too long. It was not the girls who got restless this time, but me. Once again, I found myself being completely overtaken by Ben Rutherford thoughts. How did that happen? I was convinced that I'd been put under some sort of hypnosis the first time we'd met. I mean, I didn't even like the man anymore. He had hurt me. Why would I want to give him any air time in my head?

Uncle Bob persuaded me to bring the girls to the Christening Party, which was being held at a rather posh golf club nearby. At least there would be more places for me to hide! It was hard to say "no" to that Uncle Bob smile. I agreed and we headed towards the car park together.

Then I heard his voice behind me. He was chatting to Auntie Grace. I put on my blinkers and stared straight ahead. I increased my speed to a slight canter and managed to reach my car without contact. I had done well. Now all I had to do was avoid him for two or three more hours and then my mission would be complete.

I pulled up at the golf club and took in the beautiful scenery; vast areas of plush green grass, stretching for miles, and a very smart looking building, which looked like the golf membership cost a fair few pennies.

There were lots of people entering the party. Jenna and Michael had built themselves a good network of friends with similar aged children, so the noise level was a little higher than the last christening. The great thing was that they had supplied a large soft play area in the convention room, along with a ball pool and pop-up tent. Jesse and Amy were in their element. They ran off and instantly mingled with the numerous other children, which left me free to mingle with the adults.

I was pleased to see Lucy and made my way across the room to greet her. As I did so, I saw a fast-moving man heading straight for me. There was nowhere to take cover.

"Alana", he leaned in for a kiss on the cheek. "You look beautiful, as ever."

The first thing I noticed was that he had loosened his tie and undone his top button. I wished I had not noticed that, as the sight made me a little weak and that was not in my plan at all.

"Ben, lovely to see you." I placed my hand on his arm briefly before I whisked myself away from him and continued on my determined path to Lucy. There was no way I would be stopping for a three-hour conversation with Mr. Rutherford today. I was not going to give him an opportunity to move any more furniture into his little apartment in my mind.

I couldn't quite believe I had walked away from him. I wanted to look back. In fact, to be honest, I wanted to return to that exact spot where I had heard the words "you look beautiful" but I was on a mission and I had to remember it: Operation Damage Limitation. I had to drive away from the christening with my head and mind intact; protected and secure.

That meant avoidance at all costs.

Never underestimate a woman on a mission.

CHAPTER 30

Mission Impossible

I stuck by Lucy's side for some time before the buffet food arrived. I positioned myself so that I could not scout the room for the back of his head or accidentally, on purpose, catch his eye. I knew what I was like and had learnt my lesson. As we made our way to the food, I felt his presence. Was it his gaze burning into me, or his thoughts trying to tap into my mind psychically? It was such a powerful feeling and I recognised it from our previous encounters. It was not something I felt when any other human was in the room. A possible explanation was that he was some kind of superhero but, on second thoughts, that was probably not 'possible' at all.

I took a plate from the pile and then so did he. He had snuck in the queue beside me.
  "Too much to choose from", he said, looking at the enormous spread of food. Jenna and Michael had spoilt us all.
I did not look to my left, indeed I concentrated hard on the wonderful food. Lasagne looked good; Tikka Masala; BBQ ribs. I spied chicken nuggets, so the girls would be happy.
  "I don't know where to start", I finally said, shaking my head and

smiling and before I knew it, I looked to my left and, WHAM, our eyes met and he smiled right back. I had given him an opening to continue the conversation. Why hadn't I just been rude and not answered, ignored him and walked off? I could feel myself melting, or was it just the heat from the buffet?

I hurriedly scooped up a portion of Lasagne but as I had feared, it was too late. Ben asked me how I was, how the girls were, how the business was going. As we made our way along the buffet line, the conversation was in full flow. I found myself waiting at the end of the line for him as he was answering my question and then he gestured to an empty table for us to sit down. How was that happening? I had been convinced that my willpower was at 100% when I had arrived and yet now it was in minus numbers.

As we talked, it struck me how much he remembered about my life, my friends and my world. He asked if I had been to London lately and sampled any new cocktails. With each minute that passed, my barriers came down and, within the hour, it was as if we had no awkward history at all. Nothing was mentioned about our rendezvous, or about the letters, or the birthday text. It was all just about that precious moment in time. Mission failed.

Never underestimate the power of now.

CHAPTER 31

The Last Goodbye

We spent a good hour at our table. Various friends and family joined us at times, weaving themselves into our conversations, which had flowed from one subject to another with such ease. We laughed a lot and it appeared that Ben was transfixed on me. I felt his warm eyes sparkle and he seemed to be gazing at me constantly. I was hoping I wasn't sparkling back. After all, I had completely messed up my plan to avoid him at all costs and was now in grave danger of surrendering my heart to this man yet again.

At that point, Michael announced that the grown-ups could use the golf range if we wanted to. Free balls in the baskets! I stood up immediately and said to Ben, "He doesn't have to ask me twice. I love golf." I saw a surprised look on his face, which turned into a wry smile.
"You, Alana Leevy, never cease to amaze me", and he got up out of his chair following me towards the golf range. I felt myself strut confidently in my heels in the knowledge that his eyes were still on me. "Alana, stop flirting" an internal voice reprimanded me but I was having too much fun. All rules, regulations and plans had gone

out of the window.

I checked on the girls briefly and saw that they were engrossed in a pretend tea party with various children. Auntie Grace assured me she would look after them for me.

The next hour was brilliant fun. I had to remove the heels to swing at the ball but that wasn't a problem. Ben said, "Oh, so you are not the same height as me in real life!" I laughed and loved whatever was happening between us.

I realised I was the only female who had taken up the golf range invite. I did tend to love sport, most sports, and my Dad had encouraged that in my early years. He'd taken me up to the golf range on Saturdays whenever he could, taught me the correct grip and where to keep my head during the swing. All those tips were flooding back to me and seemed to have primed me for that very moment.

The men seemed genuinely impressed and Michael was very happy to have found out my secret skill. "Alana, you'll have to come up more often, have a game with Jenna and me but she's not as good as you (don't tell her I said that!)".

The afternoon concluded with a champagne toast and Jenna and Michael made a lovely speech. I stood beside Ben and his elbow nudged me when Michael said, "It's been wonderful to have you here". I turned to look at him and smiled. On further analysis, I was not entirely sure what the nudge meant. Was it a coincidence that it had been at the point when Michael said "it's been wonderful to have you here", or was I reading too much into that? Perhaps he just lost his balance and nudged my arm accidentally. If I was honest with myself, I think it was a genuine nudge of affection. It felt like the loveliest thing in the world.

The christening party came to an end. I watched as people said goodbye to each other and started to move towards the exit. Suddenly, there was an excruciating silence. I didn't want that moment to end and yet it was forced upon us. Fortunately, at that point, my two lovely girls bounded towards me, grinning at their party bags. Some things never got old! I gave them a joint hug and was so relieved to see them; they brought me back to Mum mode and that felt much better than Hopeless Romantic mode.

Ben smiled at Jesse and Amy and, for that split second, I remembered the letter and the reasons he had given for not wanting to pursue a relationship with me. Reality check. It gave me the strength to say my goodbye.

I smiled at Ben and gave him a kiss on the cheek. "It's been lovely to see you again. Goodbye, Ben".
"Lovely to see you, too, Alana, really lovely" and he looked a little lost like he was trying to say something else but I smiled one last time and ushered my girls towards the door.

Jenna had already told me she only planned to have 2 children. There would be no more christenings. That was probably the last time I would see Ben Rutherford. It was quite possibly the last goodbye.

Never underestimate the joy of a nudge.

CHAPTER 32

Life Goes On

Sleepless nights followed the christening. Sleepless nights and restless days. My exterior carried on as normal, not uttering a single word about it to anyone, except Frankie of course, whom I'd spent an hour relaying the details to.

I smiled and laughed as usual but was wondering if I was just a big fake. After all, I was a drama teacher; a specialist in pretending to be someone else. Here I was, lying to the world; carrying on like nothing was wrong, like I was a woman in complete control. The horrible truth was, I was far from it.

It seemed that I was once again in the vicious cycle of hopelessness that engulfed me like a tidal wave after contact with Ben Rutherford. That undesirable, internal battle between dream and reality. When I returned from the christening, my mind had been full of all the wonderful detail. My heart could still feel the warmth of his affection and my arm could still imagine that little nudge. I breathed it all in. I breathed him in. I loved thinking about how special it felt to be in his company; how exciting life felt.

Then came the giant, gaping hole. For days after I felt empty. Something was missing. He was missing. Moments felt colder and less appealing. I felt less appealing.

On the fourth day came the analysing. Why was I allowing these thoughts to take over? Why was I so emotionally attached to Ben? Why couldn't I have the same emotional attachment to a man who actually wanted to be in my life? There was only one explanation that ever made sense to me:

He was The One.

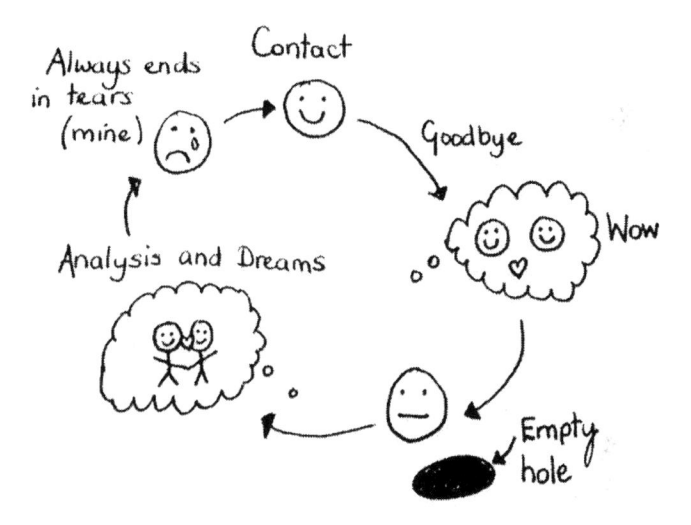

[Diagram: A cycle showing "Contact" (smiley face) → "Goodbye" → cloud with two faces labeled "Wow" → face with "Empty hole" → "Analysis and Dreams" (cloud with couple holding hands) → sad face labeled "Always ends in tears (mine)" → back to Contact]

It always came back to the same conclusion. He was the one that I was supposed to fall in love with and vice versa. We were destined, one day, for a happy ending.

I let myself dream for a few minutes about walking down a grand staircase, in a beautiful white dress, looking down to see Ben Rutherford smiling up at me with all that love in his eyes, all that sparkle that was visible only when we were together, as if Walt Disney had added some of his special effects to the characters.

Then, as soon as the dream reached the exchange of vows, I felt that internal slap yet again. I closed my eyes and sighed heavily. All that time wasted on an impossible dream; all that energy conjuring up unhelpful visions of white dresses and staircases; pointless fantasies of sparkliness. I was driving myself crazy. I decided to write in my journal:

> *"Surely, one must have the transformative power*
> *To indulge in fresh thinking*
> *Undreamed...for an hour*
> *Over-indulged and processed thoughts*
> *Stalemate of crosses and noughts*
> *Treading water, circled maze*
> *Inner chatter, wasted days*
> *A tired mind*
> *The same old line*
> *Leading to my own decline*
> *Wake me up*
> *And shake me free*
> *For I am clearly losing me"*

Never underestimate over-indulged and processed thoughts.

CHAPTER 33

Somewhere Over the Rainbow

The following day, I woke with a bit more determination to enjoy the day. I re-read the poem I'd written the night before and it still resonated with me so much. I was tired of the inner chatter; tired of the circled maze; tired of treading water; tired of the wasted days. I wanted to break free from the hopelessness of the dream, for it was a hopeless dream and I knew it.

I got ready for work. I was teaching Drama in the school 2 days a week - the volunteering work had led to a permanent position - which was good for me. I'd made a great bunch of teacher friends who had welcomed me into the team as one of their own. I was pleased to have the distraction of teaching. The weekend had not helped my troubled mind one little bit; too much time to wallow in that unhelpful pit of desperation.

At lunchtime, I met up with Adam and Caitlin in the staff room. We were laughing about something completely inappropriate when I reached into my handbag to check my phone. I was still laughing when I saw there was a message from:

BEN RUTHERFORD

My eyes shot wide open in shock. I took a sharp intake of breath and had to sit down. Adam clocked my reaction and looked concerned. "What's happened? Are you OK?" I shook myself out of the stunned look on my face.

"Yes, yes, I'm fine. Just got a text I wasn't expecting, that's all."

"Oh, yes, sounds like gossip to me." Adam raised his eyebrows in an expectant way, which meant he wanted to know more. There was something quite endearing about Adam's interest in the text and at that moment, I decided to tell him a very abbreviated and summarised version of events between Ben Rutherford and myself.

Caitlin was also on the edge of her seat when I had finished waffling on. Somehow, saying it all out loud from the beginning, it was quite a story, especially the part with the letters. Adam and Caitlin had both gasped when I said he'd eventually replied years later. It seemed as if it was a completely compelling story.

"Oh, my God! So what does he say in this text?" Adam asked eagerly.

"I have no idea. I haven't read it! I just saw his name, went weak at the knees and had to sit down. Crazy isn't it?"

"What's crazy is you haven't read the text yet." Caitlin seemed more keen than me to find out the contents of the message. There was a part of me that wished they weren't in the room anymore. I wanted to read the message in private because I had no clue what it could possibly say and so, no clue as to how I would react. It was clear that I had an expectant audience now, with front row seats. I would have to read the text right there and then.

I grabbed my phone and opened the message:

BEN – ALANA   "I've been thinking…it's not likely there will be any more christenings, so if we want to be friends, then we'll have to make our own arrangements. How about it? Would you like to have dinner one night next week? My shout."

So, there it was; a lightning bolt out of the sky. It was a miracle. I read it out loud to my audience, who were grinning broadly and Caitlin clapped excitedly.

"In other words, he wants to take you on a date", Adam said triumphantly. I was quick to discount this translation.

"It's not a date. He says 'if we want to be friends'." My evidence was strong.

"Um, Alana, guys do not ask 'friends' out for dinner. Believe me, I know these things." Adam grinned knowingly.

"I agree", Caitlin said, "he's just saying 'friend' to cover his back, in case you say no."

I took in their evidence and a little part of me jumped for joy but my commonsense kept me firmly on the ground.

"Well, I think you are both wrong on this occasion. It's not a date. Definitely not. After all that's happened, he wouldn't ask me on a date. We just get on well and I do make a pretty good friend." I smiled at Caitlin and Adam and felt that I had regained my composure and settled my beating heart.

"Well, we'll see about that Missy. If he pays for the meal, then it's definitely a date!", Adam grinned cheekily and we left the staff room.

At the end of the day, I walked home in the pouring rain, with the girls splashing in puddles beside me. I looked up and saw a double rainbow in the sky. It really was a day of miracles.

Never underestimate sharing your 'story so far'.

CHAPTER 34

Non-date Night

Many things changed after receiving the precious message. I developed a skip in my step, a renewed energy for life. I looked in the mirror more and vowed to take action on a skin-care routine. I booked a hairdresser and beautician appointment. I asked around for suggestions and reserved a table at a beautiful riverside restaurant. I bought a new skirt, slightly shorter than usual and a new pair of shoes, a little higher than usual. I invested in a fitted black and white coat, which made me look quite sophisticated. I crammed a lot of self-improvements into 7 days and, by the time Non-Date-Day came, I was feeling great.

Frankie was more excited than me and had been asking for daily updates as to how the preparations were going. She had agreed with Adam and Caitlin that it was definitely a date but I was in adamant denial that it wasn't. I knew it was denial for the benefit of the outside world because I did not want the embarrassment of having to explain to everyone if it all ended in failure, as it had before. I was also in denial to myself. It was much easier to say it was just 2 friends meeting up for a chat than have to admit that it was a date. Dates came with bundles of nerves, high emotions, complicated rules and etiquette. It was definitely not a date.

However, there was always that Disney Princess in me that swam to the surface every so often; Ariel, the mermaid. Maybe it was a date. Maybe he loved me as much as I loved him. Hang on, who said anything about love? Maybe he'd thought about me consistently since the christening and felt the same emptiness on parting company. Maybe that was the first of many dates to come. Maybe that was it. I felt nerves appear from nowhere and I pushed Ariel back under the water. I much preferred being a cynic. It wasn't a date.

I met Adam and Caitlin for a Pre-Non-Date drink.
"For someone who's not going on a date, you look stunning", Adam said as he warmly kissed my cheek.
"Do you think I should go home and change into my jeans? Is the skirt a bit too date-like?" I had contemplated the jeans and t-shirt look but the Princess in me wouldn't allow it.
"No way! You look irresistible. If it's not a date when he arrives, it soon will be when he sees you!"
I was grateful and relieved to hear the positive comments and took them with me when I drove to the riverside restaurant an hour later.

I hadn't thought much about what I would say or how we would greet each other. As I pulled into the car park, I saw his black Audi. I decided not to park next to him, or indeed, under the light. I found a nice, dark corner for 'Sylvester' to hide. Ben was not in his car. I checked my phone:

BEN – ALANA   "I'm in the bar x."

My heart flipped quite involuntarily but I ignored it. Denial. I walked across the car park and saw him standing at the bar. Second flip of the evening and I wasn't even a minute into it. I pulled the door open and entered the bar. Ben turned to look and caught my eye immediately. He held his gaze and smiled warmly. Did I detect that sparkle in his eyes again?

We had a drink at the bar while waiting for our table. We were immediately immersed in conversation; free flowing, playful chat about our week leading up to that day. I did, of course, miss out any mention of the mass hysteria amongst my friends as to whether it was a date.

I glanced at his black shirt for a millisecond, just long enough to make my heart skip another beat. That man knew how to wear a shirt; perfect fit and very stylish. He wore charcoal grey trousers, which also fitted snugly but I refused to avert my eyes to that region. There was no need to. I was merely a friend; a good one. I started to comment on the decor of the restaurant, when it happened.
 "Alana, sorry to interrupt but you look amazing. I very much like that skirt."
I grinned from ear to ear. "It likes you, too", I said, still smiling and wondering if I had just become Bridget Jones.

There was a slight awkward pause while I inwardly discussed whether I should compliment his exceptionally attractive, black shirt but fortunately, my thoughts were interrupted by a young, happy-looking waitress who was ready to show us to our table.

The evening was filled with fun, laughter, warmth and quite a lot of sparkly magic, which, although it was invisible, was certainly there. We were coming to the end of our main course when our friendly, sweet, young waitress came over to ask if we would like the dessert menu.

Ben and I looked at each other and I raised my eyebrows in a questioning manner. Ben said:

"I could force myself to eat dessert if it means the evening lasts longer."

I heard the words as I felt his eyes look into my heart and soul. I held his happy gaze and wanted the moment to last forever. Then I heard the sweet waitress ask the question:

"Are you two on a date?"

I shot back into the real world and denial quickly washed over me.

"Oh, no, we're just friends having a catch up; long story really." I was perhaps a little too animated in my cover-up. I smiled up at the waitress, who then looked embarrassed she had asked the question.

"I'm sorry, I shouldn't have asked! It's just you two look like you've enjoyed your evening more than most of the couples in here."

"You are very observant", Ben said, "if we are not on a date, we probably should be. Let's order dessert, Alana."

The waitress smiled, obviously still embarrassed about asking the question. In fact, I had never expected the question to have been asked. Perhaps Adam and Caitlin were hiding round the corner and had slipped her a fiver to find out whether it was a date or not! As I browsed the dessert menu, I tried to memorise Ben's exact words...."If we are not on a date, we probably should be." They were important words. I had detected a surprised look on Ben's face during my complete date denial with the waitress. Did all this conclude that it was a date? It was certainly feeling that way and, for the first time that evening, I felt date nerves kick in. He rescued me.

"I'm guessing you will have the vanilla cheesecake", he smiled and added, "I believe you are partial to a cheesecake." I laughed. He was quoting my own words from our previous restaurant experience.

"I am so predictable!" The awkward blip was gone. I was back to base.

All too soon, we were the last people left in the restaurant.

"Alana, you will have to stop talking; these lovely people want to go home!" Ben playfully teased as he had been the one holding conversation for the last ten minutes. I had been attentively and genuinely hooked on him while devouring my cheesecake and all time and place had been lost on me.

I went to the ladies' room and when I got back, he was standing with our coats at the bar. He held mine and helped me put my arms in. I felt like I was in an old romantic movie. He ushered me towards the door.

"Hang on, we haven't paid yet!" I gasped. I did not want to be arrested that close to home.
"I paid, silly; how could I not pay? It's been a wonderful evening of fun, great food, friendly service and exceptional company" he said warmly.
"Well, when you put it like that, thank you."
Then, there we were, under the stars, standing by his car, his arm still gently around my back.
"I've had a lovely night, thank you." I really had.
"Well, we'll have to do it again then, won't we?" He looked at me and smiled and I felt a weakness on a mass scale.
He leaned in and gave a gentle, warm kiss on the lips, not long enough to be a 'kiss' but much longer than a 'peck' "I'll be in touch." We went our separate ways.

I floated home in a happy bubble, with slightly less denial than at the start of the night. I think that may, possibly, have been a date.

Never underestimate undeniable magic.

CHAPTER 35

Crumbs

So, on the back of that most wonderful evening, my world started to sparkle again. Every little thing brought me pleasure. I felt a happiness inside which I wanted to capture and never let go. My mind meandered happily into the future, thinking of where Ben and I would go on our next date. I wandered further and further into the future and felt a contentment that I loved.

I embraced my girls with a new-found energy. It was so much easier to be a positive parent with no clouds in the sky. My heart was light and excited. There was no denying anything now. I was loved up.

"If we are not on a date, we probably should be." The words fluttered around my head, bringing a grin to my face every time. I remembered the feeling from years ago, after our first rendezvous, and yet this felt different. I was more certain, more sure of his feelings. After the comments he had made, I had no reason to doubt that he felt the same as me.

Until, of course, the silence fell. Again. Ben had sent a text the day after 'The Date' to say:

BEN – ALANA   "Great evening last night. We will do it again soon x."
and I had replied:

ALANA – BEN   "It really was lovely. Have a great week. Let me know when you are free and we'll arrange something x."

The days totted up on a tally... lllll lllll 10 days. Nothing. I tried to be cool. Maybe, we'd meet next month. We were both busy; we didn't want to impact too much on our schedules but inside, I knew.
My happy heart balloon was deflating fast. I tried desperately to keep the positive air in but I just knew, and one evening I slumped into bed, aware that my happiness was gone.

I was recycling old emotions; confusion and disappointment re-entered at No. 1 and No. 2 in the Emotion Charts. What was going on? I looked at my phone and decided to make the next move:

ALANA – BEN   "Hi, Ben. Hope work is not too busy. I'm starting to feel the need for cheesecake. Would you like to join me x?"

It was light-hearted but friendly and direct. I felt sure he would reply to it. Perhaps he had just been busy at work.

However, the silence continued and with every day and every tally made lllll lllll lllll lllll I was struck down deeper. My self-esteem plummeted until, on the 20th day:

BEN – ALANA   "Alana, all good here, thanks. Hope this text finds you well, too x."

So, there it was; the reply. The reply I had been longing for. 10 days

late and 10 times less exciting than I had hoped for; 10 times more damaging to my self-esteem than no reply at all; 10 times more confusing than silence.
I decided to write 10 lines in my journal that night:

> I must never 'date' Ben Rutherford again
> I must never 'date' Ben Rutherford again, etc

A written punishment was definitely needed. I had clearly not learnt my lesson from years ago. I had been sucked in yet again, quite convincingly, to believe I stood a chance with him. I was now back to that horrible square one. I was annoyed that he had, yet again, instigated a 'date'; I was annoyed that I had knocked down my barriers and let him in; I was annoyed that I had believed every word he said that evening; I was annoyed that I had believed in the invisible, sparkly magic thing; I was annoyed that I now had to do a whole heap of journalistic therapy to move on from this day; I was annoyed but mostly, I was hurt.

> *"Acceptance never comes*
> *As you drop your love in crumbs"*

Never underestimate the power of ten.

CHAPTER 36

Settling

I will try to summarise the next two years after that confusing but massively hurtful rejection by Ben. I had confided in Frankie and the others, partaking in the usual 'pick yourself up' ritual of going out and everyone telling me "he doesn't deserve you", "he's an idiot for letting you go", so that by the end of the evening, his ears must have been burning like the sun. Friends didn't hold back.

I heard the words and outwardly, I agreed wholeheartedly that he was an 'idiot', although inside, I didn't agree. Inside, I had a firm belief that he did feel the same way as me, that he felt the connection but he was holding himself back for two reasons:

1. I was not good enough for him (status, education, wealth, intelligent vocabulary).
2. I had two children he did not want to get involved with.

If I had honestly felt bitterness towards him, it would have been a better place to be. Instead, it was an incredibly sad place to be.

I had found the one person in the world who lit up my heart, who excited me about life and who I felt I could have dinner with every night and not ever get bored and yet, he would not let himself love me.

Perhaps, he was a love rat; perhaps he was a serial dater, ripping the hearts out of women. That was Malia's theory. Perhaps he was a control freak, having to call the shots; Natalia's theory. Perhaps he was married to his job; Frankie's theory. He could quite possibly have been all these things but they had not been sitting opposite him at that restaurant. They had not felt his warmth or looked into his eyes. If they had, I think they would have backed me up on my theory.

Sadness was a lonely place and with sadness, comes vulnerability. With vulnerability, comes bad choices. Then Joshua appeared.

I could indeed write an entire novel on this relationship alone, but then that would be side-tracking from the job at hand. It was, however, to be a very significant relationship for all the wrong reasons.

Joshua was a good man, a kind man and a man looking for a ready-made family, who had similar interests to me, whom I could converse with easily and a man who desperately wanted to be a dad/step dad. He was an instant texter; no waiting around for 20 days for a pointless reply; he was reliable, always there. He was a friend of a friend.

Looking back, I could see the pitfalls, see where I was headed but, at the time, I was a sad, demoralised young woman who had fought off evil in a devastating marriage, only to rebuild some kind of confidence, only to be smashed into pieces by an unrequited love.

When Joshua found me, I was on the emotional floor, needing to be picked up and there he was. His kind and generous ways captured my attention and I was grateful for it.

<u>Grateful:</u> feeling or showing an appreciation of kindness; thoughtful.

Here was this person who did not think he was above me in the ranks. In fact, he thought I was above him and who wanted to know all about my children, as he was ready to accept them into his life. These seemed to be the two most important boxes to tick because they were the boxes that Ben Rutherford had left unchecked.

It was not long before my girls met Joshua and were instantly taken with his kindness and attention. Perhaps they were also grateful for a good man in their lives at last. Bonds were formed and I watched them altogether and felt an appreciation, which softened my heart. It softened my heart, which I mistook for love. He fitted into my social world; the missing piece of the jigsaw puzzle. He was a friend of a friend and so, there was an instant celebration among the crowds that this was all 'meant to be'. Desperately, I tried to believe that, with every inch of my body, in the two years that followed.

'This is what you should be happy with.' 'This is the best thing for your girls.' 'Stop being so picky'. 'Be grateful for this love of a good man.' 'Try harder to feel more love.' 'It will get better.' 'You will grow to love him.' 'He is so kind and loving, you cannot break his heart.' 'Everyone thinks we are so right for each other, it's me that has the problem.' 'Be grateful, Alana, that you are loved.'

In those two years, I had 4 texts from Ben Rutherford: Christmas 2005; birthday 2006; Christmas 2006; birthday 2007. In those two years, my heart only flipped 4 times. It did not flip when I looked into Joshua's eyes. It didn't flip when he came home from work. It did not even flip when he scooped my girls up and spun them around. The only time my heart flipped was when I saw <u>his</u> name on my phone.

BEN – ALANA: "Alana, Merry Xmas. Keep being you xx."
BEN - ALANA: "Happy Birthday, Alana. Have the best day. You deserve it xx."

BEN – ALANA: "Xmas again already? Sending love to you xx."

BEN - ALANA: "Happy Birthday. Bet you look as young as ever! Have a great day xx."

There they were, 4 little crumbs. There I was, little Gretel scampering after them like a desperate hungry child. Sitting alone and immersing myself in the moment, thinking that crumb was the best thing I'd ever tasted, relishing every happy emotion running through my body but then afterwards, feeling the hunger return worse than ever. A mere crumb was not enough but it's all he would give. I had to remind myself that it was all he would ever give. Joshua was offering more than crumbs; he was offering an entire baker's shop; baguettes, bloomers and even cream cakes. He was offering his world.

I did not understand why my heart could not flip for him. Why was I so damned convinced that Ben was the love of my life? Why did it want to attach itself to such a complex, difficult man?

It was in the second year of the relationship with Joshua that I realised to my dismay what I had done. I had 'settled'. I had settled for a man I was not 'in love' with, whom I did not 'adore', whom I was not even 'attracted' to and I had done that because I was 'grateful' for his love and attention. He had come along with a big basket of it when I was starved of love and I had grabbed it with both hands in a desperate attempt to put my world back together.

But in that stark and depressing realisation, my world shattered again. Joshua would never be Ben and I would never be in love with Joshua. What had I done?

Never underestimate the damage of settling.

CHAPTER 37

The Decline

When the inevitable break-up happened, Joshua did break up, into tiny little pieces. I had shattered his world, the world he had so overwhelmingly built around us and, although none of my actions were intended to hurt him, it did not matter, because it was a sad reality that I broke his heart.

All the demons of my marriage had raised their ugly heads in the lead-up to the separation and I felt like I was dealing with two failed relationships all at the same time. I was an internal, tangled ball of string, attached to all kinds of unhelpful emotions.

Yet, on the surface, I was a survivor. I had to be for my beautiful girls. They were also broken-hearted about leaving Joshua and there was no other explanation I could give them other than: "Sometimes grown-ups just can't live with each other anymore." It was a feeble and weak explanation. I knew that but how could I transfer all my unhappiness onto them? The fact was I couldn't. So the 'everyday' went on and with even more determination than ever that their lives should be rich in love, fun, friendship and the odd McDonalds fast food treat. They were quick to adapt and accept the change, although I knew it had been a damaging experience and I hated that I'd put them through it.

There were other negative, knock-on effects from the break-up. I lost a friend, Annabelle. The 'friend of a friend' situation was not so rosy during a break-up. In fact, it was awful. I understood the loss. She had every right to think I had been a letdown and hurt Joshua with my actions. So, I accepted the harsh words that she issued one day to my face and the cold stares and sudden lack of invites to parties and events of our joint friends. It was all part of my punishment. I deserved it. I didn't fight it, as I had no strength for anything apart from keeping my outside me functioning perfectly for Jesse and Amy. That was my sole focus. Yet, with the loss of one group of friends, I soon realised that I had many others who were not so quick to judge me; who were not so entangled in the Joshua/Alana Love Web. Their kindness and understanding went far beyond anything I expected. Frankie and the girls, of course, were with me every step, making me laugh and Frankie said to me:

"I was never really sure about Joshua. I don't think he was right for you." It was a short phrase but it meant the world to me.

Caitlin, Adam and many others from the school rallied round and I was invited to fun events. They dried my tears regularly at the end of the night, when I let out all my sadness, courtesy of Pinot Grigio. They seemed to have a never-ending supply of tissues, patience and warm hugs; friendship of the highest quality.

Scarlet was also an ever increasingly special friend, making me laugh on even the darkest days and expertly guiding me professionally. We would often laugh and laugh about ridiculous inside jokes and sometimes these would be enough to save me from my most torturous thoughts.

I grieved a lot for the loss of my friendship with Annabelle. Losing a friend was somehow more painful than losing the love and affection of Joshua. The fact that she thought so badly of me cut into my soul and my self esteem and I plummeted to an all-time low.

Yet, with all that had happened, I knew that, deep down, I was not a bad person. I was just a completely messed-up person who did not know what to do; did not know what to think and did not know what the hell she was doing with her life. The outside Alana had little connection with the inside one and vice versa. I was disconnected. I needed help. I was lost.

The moment I heard myself say that I needed help, I knew it was true. I felt like I was losing my mind one day at a time. Not on the outside, but very definitely on the inside. I needed to talk to someone. So I searched the internet for counsellors and I clicked on the first one I saw. It was a clinic with multiple therapists to choose from. I scanned the names. 'Sarah Parker'; she sounded as good as any. I clicked the link to email her and typed through my tears;

"I don't know if counselling is the answer but I feel lost and I need to find myself again. I need help. Alana."

I did need help and the more I admitted it to myself, the faster my tears flowed. Within 30 minutes, Sarah Parker replied:

"You have taken the first step. Well done. Here are my free appointments this week. When can you come and see me?"

Emails to'd and fro'd, until Tuesday 4pm was in the diary. I only had to wait 48 hours. I felt a sudden wave of calm sweep over me. I had an appointment.

The next day, an invitation dropped through the letterbox. An invitation to Juliette's christening. I stared at it for a long time. The invitation would quite possibly take me back to that world where Ben Rutherford would be; where we would talk and laugh and I would feel alive but that was the last thing I needed right now. It was no longer about Ben Rutherford; it was no longer about Joshua; this was about me. So, I declined the invitation politely and decided to stay well away from him.

On Tuesday, I would have my first session with Sarah Parker and I knew it would take up all my energy.

Never underestimate that little voice inside that says "I need help".

CHAPTER 38

Piercings, Bare Feet and Water

The first time I sat in the little waiting room, I could feel my heart beating faster. I scanned the numerous 'help' leaflets for various mental health issues, flicked through ancient copies of 'Heat Magazine', celebrating the marriage of a celebrity couple who were now divorced and fidgeted awkwardly with nerves.

I looked out of the big, old window and into the garden, which had me transfixed. It was large and entangled in various overgrown weeds, intertwined and confused. Among the weeds were some beautiful old trees, looking wise and unbothered by the mess beneath them. It needed a good sorting out and I suddenly became very connected to that garden. I, too, needed sorting out. I was still looking out of the window when I heard the soft patter of feet on the stairs. I looked to the door and that's when I first saw Sarah Parker. I had envisaged her to be in her 40's smartly dressed, with glasses that she would wear down her nose and peer over at me. That to me was Sarah Parker. However, I was a little confused. She was maybe in her early 30's, had plaited hair, on second glance they appeared to be dreads, a nose piercing and a fair few ear piercings, too.

"Alana, so good to meet you. My room's upstairs, if you'd like to follow me."

I wasn't sure I did want to. I suddenly felt extremely awkward and my pre-judgements had been so wrong that it had thrown me off balance. I felt the temperature rise in my cheeks and involuntarily, my breathing became shallow. Somehow my legs politely obeyed this unexpected lady and I followed Sarah Parker up the stairs, only to realise that she was not wearing any shoes. More to the point, she was not wearing any socks either.

I suddenly wondered if I had clicked on the 'Hippy Counselling Service' and berated myself for not researching more carefully. I seemed to remember I had chosen this woman at random. I crossed my fingers tightly in the hope that her room was not full of incense and candles. I could not deal with incense.

Sarah Parker opened the door and welcomed me into her room, which, to my absolute relief, did not look like a Hippy room at all. In fact, it was a lovely, light but plain-looking room with two chairs by the window. She gestured towards the seats and I gratefully sat down.

"Please help yourself to water and take a minute to rest. Those stairs can sometimes feel like a very long journey."

Indeed, I had managed to have an in-depth conversation with myself during those two flights of steps. It *had* felt like a long journey.

Sarah Parker sat cross-legged on her chair and waited patiently for me to sip my water. I awkwardly sipped far longer than I needed to but if I stopped sipping, I knew I'd have to speak and I wasn't sure I was able to.

"Take your time, Alana. There is no rush. You are here; that is your first big step."

I did not know how she could read my mind. Her words comforted

me. I did not have to rush. I eventually put down my empty glass and she reached over and refilled it. As she did so, I glanced out of the large window. It was a view of the same garden, only from two floors up. It was easier to see the weeds and flowers from up there; a clearer perspective. After what seemed like a long time, I finally said:
"I like the garden."
Sarah smiled and for the first time, I took a moment to really look at

her. She had a sweet face and a genuine smile, in between the silver attached to her. I had been shocked by the piercings and bare feet because I had my own pre-conceptions. I was calming down now and I realised I had been far too quick to judge.

"I need to take down a few details in our first session and explain a few things about my role and what you can expect from me. Is it OK if we do that now?" Sarah Parker asked softly.

"Of course", I said with enormous relief. I wanted to talk about my full name and date of birth, my address and listen to rules and regulations. Maybe that would take up the full 45 minute session, so that I wouldn't have to talk about my problematic mind which was about to explode with stress.

Alas, the details and regulations were dealt with in a matter of 10 minutes, which left a whole half an hour ahead of me to talk. I did not know where to start.

"Often it is hard to know where to start." Sarah Parker was a true professional. Was she tapped into my internal chatter? It comforted me and unnerved me at the same time.

"I really don't know where to start." I shook my head and looked down into my lap. I felt heavy. Tears welled up and a single tear released itself from my tight grip. Sarah Parker handed me a quality Kleenex and said, "I have an endless supply." I took it gratefully and when I had caught the loose tear, I clenched the tissue tightly in my palm to use as a stress ball.

I glanced out of the window and eventually said:

"I feel like that garden; I'm in a total mess; I've got deep-rooted problems; I haven't looked after myself in years; I've looked after my girls, they are my world, but I'm crumbling inside and if I don't do something about it, I will be no good to them. I need help because I'm so sad."

Sarah Parker nodded with what looked like empathy. Perhaps, she had been in a garden similar to mine. I trusted her in that moment. "Alana, most people never realise they need to step into a room like this. Most people are never brave enough to. You have been brave to come here today. The thing about messy gardens is that, with hard work and effort, they can be transformed into places of peace, tranquility and beauty. I would like to work with you to help you."

My first session with Sarah Parker was definitely not plain sailing; it was filled with fraught, internal emotion and it made me shake with tension and fear but I walked out of the big, old house, knowing I would turn up at the same time the following week because I knew it was going to help. Sarah Parker and her bare feet were going to help me find myself.

Never underestimate how wrong first impressions can be.

CHAPTER 39

Christening (No Show)

The day of the christening came. It was a very odd day; I felt as if my mind was there at the church, looking around for him, yet my body was well and truly a million miles away. In fact, with all the emotional turmoil I put myself through that day, I might just as well have attended.

My confidence was nowhere to be found, so I was pleased to be curled up with my girls on the sofa, watching a film. My hair and skin were lifeless, dry and dull. My body felt heavy, weighed down and slow. The stress of my inside was definitely manifesting itself into physical form on the outside.

I had lost count of the times people had said "Alana, you look so...tired." Even my girls asked, "Are you tired, Mum? You look tired." I would brush off the comments light-heartedly, claiming to have woken up too early or gone to bed too late, but the truth was I was incredibly tired; tired of feeling tired; tired of battling with my emotions; tired of feeling low; tired of struggling with money; tired of dark clouds in my sky. I looked tired because I was tired. The only energy I seemed to have was enough to just get me through the day;

to go to work; to look after my girls and that's all I could manage. Except, of course, on Tuesdays. I always needed a lot more energy on Tuesdays, because I went to see Sarah Parker.

I had been going to counselling now for 4 weeks and discovered that the first session, that difficult day, had actually been a piece of cake in comparison to what followed.

"Counselling is a very individual process", Sarah Parker had explained. The session would be controlled by me but whatever came up, she would help me through it. At first, this scared me almost enough to stop me turning up at my second appointment. That same thought always came to me, "Where did I start? How did I work out when my life came tumbling down around me? How do I know when my heart broke and shattered into tiny pieces?"

I forced myself, with every inch of my willpower, to attend the second session. I smiled weakly when I heard Sarah's bare feet coming down the stairs to greet me and I kept my smile and said a quiet "hello". The stairs felt like a long trek again and I wondered, for the 19th time that day whether counselling was for me.
I took a quick look out of the window at the entangled garden and somehow it looked even more of a mess than before. I sat in my chair, drank my water and then glanced over at Sarah, who looked softer that day. Maybe, it was the red jumper she had on. It suited her.

"You made it, Alana, well done", Sarah said, with her sweet, caring smile.

"I nearly didn't make it. I nearly stayed at home. I nearly went for a coffee. I was nearly anywhere but here." I took a deep breath and closed my eyes, as a tear was already forming in my eye.

"But you did make it and you are here. And you are safe." Sarah Parker nudged the box of tissues a little closer to me. It was clear I was going to need them.

In that second session, I decided to take Maria Von Trappe's advice:
  "Let's start at the very beginning
  A very good place to start"

I began at the point when I first met Ian, the girls' father, and went through events in a kind of timeline manner. That way, I had a structure to work from and it made it slightly easier to decide what I would talk about.

So, I started at the beginning, which, in itself, was OK. I talked about how it felt to be loved by a man, to be complimented, to feel pretty and the feelings of hope for a happy future. Sarah Parker would often say:

  "And how did that make you feel?"

I would stop and try to remember how it felt. At first, the relationship had brought me happiness and had given me confidence, something I had lacked on several levels as a teenager. Here was this older man interested in 'me', wanting to give his attention to 'me' and wanting to build his life with 'me'.

The third session made me realise something profound. I heard myself saying:

  "I am not the same person as I was back then."

Sarah Parker asked me to explain more.
  "I feel that when I talk about the past, it's like it happened to someone else. The choices I made back then, the things that happened, it's just not me."
Sarah Parker explained, "It was 'you'. It was 'you' but at the age of 17; a young woman at the start of her adult life. It was Alana with all the hopes of an excited young woman, trusting and naive. Alana at

30, with years more experience is looking back and instead of brushing young Alana to one side, locking her away and everything attached to her, it is time to listen to her; time to heal her pain; time to reconnect with her because until you do, you may feel disconnected with yourself. She is part of you. She matters."

I listened to Sarah's words and they resonated with me. Young Alana was part of me still, and no matter how hard I tried, I could not erase her. I could not erase that time of my life.
"So, how do I heal her?" I asked
"You listen to her. You let her speak. You try to understand her. You give her time and love and then you connect with her. You let her be part of you and stop trying to run away from her."
It was true. I had been running from her. I hadn't wanted to think about her for the last 9 years. I had wanted to leave her in Manchester. But it made sense. She was still crying inside me. She needed to heal.

That is when I truly understood why I needed counselling. I had to listen to the young Alana.

So, as I sat there on the day of the Christening, curled up and cuddling my girls, I had two trails of thought racing through my head:
"I wonder if Ben Rutherford has noticed I'm missing" and "on Tuesday, I will work hard to connect with the young Alana."
I missed Ben Rutherford that day. I knew it had been a chance for my heart to miss a beat, an opportunity to spend an hour happily chatting and being transported to a world where I felt like somebody I wanted to be. Perhaps, I had just missed the last opportunity to see him. The thoughts went on and on and on. I wondered if his ears would be burning with my telepathic thoughts. I would never know.

Never underestimate reconnecting with your past self.

CHAPTER 40

Friend Request

About a month later, I had a conversation with Frankie and the girls about Facebook. I'd heard various snippets of information about the 'social networking' site from other friends but I hadn't taken much notice. Natalia and Jodie encouraged Frankie and me to sign up, after a couple of Pinot's at Frankie's new apartment.

There was an air of excitement about it. We were soon connected to friends and friends of friends, looking at pictures of babies, holidays and searching for long lost school acquaintances.
 "Who do you want to look up, Alana?" Frankie raised her eyebrows at me inquisitively.
I made a puzzled face and lied, "I can't think of anyone!" Why, when faced with this situation, was there only one person I wanted to search for? One man I wanted to see pictures of. My mind wandered to him yet again and that dull ache entered my heart, thoughts of him buzzing round my head.

I found myself in that half-in/half-out place, when my outside functioned on automatic, laughing at the right times and smiling but inside, I was distracted. It was like someone had turned a tap on in my brain and left it running; love was flowing inside me and

I wonder if he's single?

I wonder if he thinks about me?

I wonder if he's happy?

drowning out everything else.
I finally decided to get Frankie to search for Jenna. Within minutes, she had been excitedly found and requested. By morning, she had accepted and posted a lovely message on my wall:

"Welcome, Alana, to the wonderful world of Facebook. Love you x."

The message made me really smile. It was my first social networking communication and I instantly liked it.

The last few months had been a dark and difficult time and all of a sudden, I felt a little bit better. I had connected to my London Girls over wine and Facebook and I was now connected to lovely Jenna. I had slept over at Frankie's and we had chatted all morning about life, the universe and Ben Rutherford. She talked about how happy she was with Jenson and then I looked at the time.

"I'd better get back. I said to Mum and Dad I'd be home by lunchtime. Jesse and Amy always watch the clock when I'm gone!"
I went to the bathroom and as I was brushing my teeth, Frankie called out:

"Ooh, you've got a friend request come through on the laptop!"
I finished off my ablutions and opened the door eagerly. I skipped

over to the laptop and clicked on the 1 friend request highlighted.

"Who's it from?" Frankie asked as she washed up our cups of tea. I stared at the screen and raised my eyebrows involuntarily. There he was, his warm eyes looking straight at me. "Ben Rutherford", I said, in a slightly calmer voice than expected.

"Ben Rutherford!!!? Are you kidding me?"
Frankie left the sink, dripping soapy water all over her new carpet.
"Let me see!!!!"
I double clicked on his profile picture and there he was, in double size. Frankie opened her mouth wide with excitement and then said;

"You two are like Charles and Camilla; it might not happen yet but I think it will one day!" and she strolled back to the sink. "So, are you going to accept his friend request?"

"Maybe", I said casually. But we both knew that was a sure-fire 'yes'.

Never underestimate making somebody double sized.

CHAPTER 41

Accepted

My drive home that day was noisy. My brain was unsettled from the unexpected friend request. I tried blasting Capital Radio through the speakers but it did not drown out the persistent inner chatter. I could not deny the skipped heartbeat and the excitement welling up inside me. HE had friend requested ME. The noisy chatter continued when I arrived home. Jesse and Amy bounded towards me and excitedly caught me up on every second I had missed while I had been away.

"Mum, my tooth is even more wobbly now, look!" Jesse yanked her tooth as evidence. Then Amy butted in, "I fell over Mummy and hurt my knee." I struggled to see the barely pink patch and she looked slightly put out that the mark had faded! I listened attentively to my beautiful girls but there was a constant background noise still filling my head. In fact, by bedtime, I felt irritable. I needed to be by myself. For some strange reason, I wanted to indulge in the excitement, in that hopeful moment, with the new knowledge that Ben Rutherford had thought about me enough to request my friendship on Facebook.

When the girls went to sleep, I went to bed, in my little box room, and sat with the laptop open, fired up and ready for action. What action should I take? I spent another half an hour thinking up witty, flirty paragraphs of words I wanted to say to him. Then the mood changed to hopeless romantic; "My heart skipped a beat when I saw your name." It was true but how could I put that? In the end, I just clicked on the Accept Friend Request icon and waited. I waited a few seconds before clicking on his profile and browsing the few posts he had made.

There was an "I've joined Facebook" status; a photo of Ben with a group of friends, sitting around a dinner table and a photo of Ben with a stunningly beautiful, European-looking woman. My eyes were transfixed on that picture. They were stood close together, side by side, with a beaming smile on both their faces. Ben looked like the cat that got the cream, and looking at the picture, maybe he had! I started to wonder who the woman was. She must be of some significance if he'd posted the picture. Maybe, she was his girlfriend. Of course, it was inevitable he had a girlfriend. He was the ultimate catch. I studied her face closely. Although on first sight, I had seen beauty, on second look, and third, and fourth, I felt she looked a bit cold. It was not a warm, friendly smile but somehow an 'I know I'm beautiful' smile. I was not sure I liked her.

I spent far too long studying the photo and far too long thinking about whether Ben and the mystery woman were an item. I tried to distract myself with sleep but sleep did not appear. I tossed and turned and wondered again why Ben triggered such high emotions in me. Firstly, it had been huge excitement from the friend request and now I was experiencing huge turmoil over one single photo that was absolutely none of my business. I could feel myself spiraling down in slow motion, falling again into to a muddled mess; thoughts of Ben entangling me. There was no other explanation. He was the love of my life; The One. Once again, I wondered why my love story was going so wrong. Most people I knew had found the love of their lives and were either happily married or living together and there was me, alone, torturing myself over a single photograph. It did not seem at all fair.

Maybe, I shouldn't have accepted the friend request after all. I had been strong and determined not to go to the christening because I knew it would do me no good to see him again and yet, the minute he showed up online, I snapped his arm off with my acceptance. If I was truthful to myself, all I wanted to do was send him a message and communicate with him. The man I loved for some unknown reason. I had all this love for him in my heart, but it seemed that he had all the love he needed right beside him in Miss Europe.

Never underestimate the damage of analysing photos on Facebook.

CHAPTER 42

A Visit from Ofsted

So, I resisted the temptation to message Ben for all of 24 hours and then, my "what the hell" voice took over and bullied me towards my laptop. If I didn't message him, I would never know if she was his girlfriend or not. I took a deep breath and started typing:

"Hi, Ben. Thanks for the friend request. Good to see you (online!). How are things with you? I couldn't make it to the christening last week, as I had another commitment. Jenna said it all went very well, apart from Juliette screaming her head off when the water crossed! Life is good here; work is getting quite busy and I've also taken on an extra job working 2 afternoons in a school teaching drama. The girls are doing well; both taken up dancing and enjoying it very much. I'm not sure either of them will be the next Darcey Bussell but you never know! I'm on Facebook now, as you can probably tell. I got bullied into joining by my girl friends the other night and I'm afraid that one too many Pinots didn't help! I will hopefully get the hang of it by next year.
Anyway, how's the job going? And the love life? Mine has been a bit

turbulent recently and I'm newly single but it was the right move. Hope to hear from you soon. Alana x."

I pressed send before I had a chance to re-read, re-phrase, delete, start again, make it shorter or not send it at all. I knew what I was like when it came to Ben Rutherford. I over-analysed everything. It was later that evening when I read the message back to myself, I realised that it sounded quite upbeat. One particular line stood out to me as a complete and utter lie:
"Life is good here."

I wondered where I had pinched that line from, a standard phrase that a lot of people use, but when I looked at it, I frowned. Things were not that good. If I was doing an Ofsted report on my life, it would probably come back 'Unsatisfactory', with a few elements of satisfactory or outstanding:

- Mental Health: (Unsatisfactory)
    *Weekly counselling to deal with past issues.
    *Unhealthy Obsession with 'THE ONE', wasting countless hours hopelessly daydreaming about a possible future relationship.

- Money: (Unsatisfactory)
    *Never quite enough money to pay bills AND have a life. Always just seem to be paying bills.

- Physical Health: (Unsatisfactory)
    *Lifeless hair
    *Bad skin

- Friends & Family: (Outstanding)
    *Supportive friends and family
    *Beautiful girls

- <u>Work</u>: (Satisfactory)
  *Good start but not enough time allocated to make drama lessons grow.
  *New job brings more money in but drains energy already lacking.
  *Good relationships with friends/colleagues.

If Ofsted had also done a 2-day observation on my life, they would clearly have put me in Special Measures. Life was far from good. It felt unsatisfactory. How had I produced such a happy-sounding message from such an unsatisfactory outlook? Perhaps, it was just the effect that Ben Rutherford always seemed to have on me. He always lifted me up somehow, to be the person I would rather be, that perhaps I was destined to be, but was failing to be at that moment in time. While I had been typing, I had been transported to the world of 'Me and Ben'; 'Ben and Me'; a better place; a happier place but now I was back to reality. If I didn't buck my ideas up, Ofsted might even close me down. I decided to call a meeting with me, myself and I with my journal at 10.00pm that night, to try to address some of the issues from the damning report.

Never underestimating saying "Life is good" when it's not.

CHAPTER 43

Cancelled Meeting

I was ready, with pen in hand, a glass of water, my journal and my troubled thoughts, at 9.48pm. I decided to put off the meeting for a few more minutes and clicked on my new favourite icon – Facebook. Frankie had sent me a text to say she had scanned in some old pictures of us and to check them out.

As I clicked on my profile, I saw, at the top of the screen, that I had 1 message. I looked at it for a second and my heart skipped a beat. Was it a reply from Ben already? I opened my Inbox and, sure enough, there was Ben Rutherford's name. He had replied!
I read the message and with every sentence, my smile got bigger:

"Dear Alana,

How wonderful to hear from you. I confess that I did miss you at the christening. I have to say that, as lovely as Bob and Grace are, I did not find them as scintillating company as you.

Glad to hear that life is good; excellent news about the new job and that your girls are blossoming. It must be because they have such a

great Mum!
Work is ever busy for me; I have recently been promoted and so seem to forever be in meetings which drag on but we seem to be making good progress so I cannot complain.

I have recently bought a holiday property in the South of France, which I am in love with. I am hoping to spend some time out there soon, away from the London rat-race.

I am due to be working near Reading soon and wondered if you have time to come out for dinner next Wednesday? It would be great to see you again.

Love from Ben xx"

I read the message five more times and as I had done with my own message, I focused on one particular line...

"I confess that I did miss you at the christening..."

My heart soaked up the words and danced in this new knowledge. He had missed me. Perhaps, my telepathic thoughts had worked! And, more than that, he had missed my scintillating company. Scintillating! I would never have known it was spelt like that. It was my new favourite word. I looked it up:

<u>Scintillating: adjective</u>
1. Sparkling or shining brightly. Synonyms: sparkling, shining bright, brilliant, gleaming, twinkling
2. Brilliantly and excitingly clever or skilful. Synonyms: brilliant, dazzling, exciting, exhilarating,, shimmering.

I focused on this word for so long and felt a huge surge of happiness enter my soul. Was I scintillating? I didn't feel like it at all but perhaps I was? Frankie always said I was great company and made her laugh and I guess there was some other evidence to support it but not much. I certainly hadn't felt at all scintillating since the break up with Joshua but perhaps there was now hope. Perhaps I could find a way to be sparkly and brilliant.

I loved Ben Rutherford for giving me this hopeful moment. I had needed it more than he would ever know. I finally re-read the end of the email. He wanted to take me to dinner. I had been here before but it didn't seem to matter. I typed my reply:

"I would love to go to dinner next Wednesday. Just let me know what time and where; really looking forward to it. Love from Alana xx."

Needless to say, I missed the emergency meeting with myself. It did not seem necessary now. After all, I'd just had the most wonderful message from Ben Rutherford and, for the first time in a long while, I felt quite outstanding.

Never underestimate being scintillating.

CHAPTER 44

Wednesday

It had been 10 days since the message had come through to brighten my world. I had told Frankie, Malia, Scarlet and Caitlin about the upcoming dinner date but I had kept the gossip close to my chest. I had learnt my lesson; better to keep it all under wraps in case nothing else came of it.

Frankie was beyond excited. She was already 'buying her hat', an expression she often used when talking about Ben and me. I loved her hopefulness. I thought she might have tried to talk me out of going, after the last Ben disaster, but all she said was, "Life's too short. Have fun and report back!"

As I was readying myself for the big evening, a thought entered my head, not for the first time either. I had noticed on re-reading the message (numerous times) that Ben had completely avoided the love-life question. I wondered why? If he was single, surely he would have made a similar comment to me. If he was attached, surely he would have said and would not be offering to take me to dinner. I came to the conclusion that Ben was just quite a private man and perhaps, he just didn't like to say. All the same, it slightly bothered me.

It also bothered me that he'd bought a holiday home in the South of France and the woman in the photo looked decidedly French. Could there be a connection? It was quite a feasible line of enquiry. The thought deflated me until I stopped myself going flat. The fact was, whatever his situation, he was taking ME out for dinner and perhaps all would become clear.

I decided to wear a red skirt and black top, my hair down and some silver accessories. Thankfully, I felt good when I looked in the mirror. His message had magical powers on my lifeless hair; it had begun to shine again.

'Just enjoy yourself', I whispered in the mirror.

We agreed to meet in town, where there was a variety of restaurants to choose from. As I approached the bridge where we had arranged to meet, I saw his silhouette against the bright lights. His strong, confident stance had been one of the first things I had noticed about him. It set him apart from everyone I had ever met, along with his warm smile that greeted me. He wore an expensive-looking black coat with the collar up and it made him look even more handsome than I had remembered.

He kissed me on both cheeks and I immediately wondered if that was a French influence; paranoia creeping in already? I felt his hand lightly touch the small of my back, as his lips brushed my cheek and electricity/chemistry/attraction, whatever you want to call it, exploded in my whole body.

It was a romantic scene with the lights glistening on the river and this handsome man beside me. We instantly struck up the rapport that seemed to always be there. Time and distance had passed but we jumped back into our world within seconds. We quickly agreed on a fine steak restaurant and before we knew it, were seated with a flickering candle between us on the table.

"It's so good to see you, Alana. You look great." He smiled into my eyes and I smiled right back.

"And you are as handsome as ever." We browsed the starter menu and ordered some drinks.

It amazed me how we could just talk and talk, flitting from one conversation to another, like a cleverly written script. We both added humour and stories and there were many smiles and clinks of glasses, as we celebrated events and various triumphs, like the purchasing of the property in France and my new job. As the subject had turned quite naturally to France, I took the plunge:

"So why France then, Ben?" I saw his expression change ever so slightly as if, for the first time, he was having to stop and think what to say.

"I fell in love with France last year." I read between the lines.

"You mean you fell in love with someone in France?" I raised my eyebrows in an inquisitive but friendly way. "Come on, you can tell me. We've known each other long enough." We had known each other for 7 years now and, although there had been many ups and downs and confusion, I felt incredibly close to him in that moment. Ben looked down and nervously rearranged his place mat.

"Well, yes, and no." He looked at me and then took a sip of his wine. He had made the decision to get the train that evening and perhaps he had known he would need a drink. I smiled across at him.

"Yes and No? Mmm that sounds confusing!"

"It is, Alana. It is." He shook his head and for the first time that evening, I saw a look of stress on his face. I wanted to take him in my arms and make him feel better, even though he appeared to be somewhat confusingly in love with someone else.

"Why is it confusing? Tell me. It might help."

"It's confusing because I thought I was in love with her. I really did. We had a whirlwind romance and I wanted her to stay at my home here in England but, well, I'm just not sure anymore."

"You are not sure you love her?"

"I'm not sure of anything. Some days I think I do, as she is a very beautiful woman. Any man would be crazy to let her go. But I don't know, sometimes she just seems cold. I don't know how to put it. I fell head over heels, only to find out she was not who I thought she was."

I could not quite believe that I had been spot on with my photo analysis. Perhaps this could be a new career route for me; private detective.

"So, she is living with you now, here in England?" The reality of the situation was sinking in.

"Yes, she is, but will be returning to France soon."

"To live in your new French apartment?"

The pieces of the puzzle were slowly fitting together.

"But you are not sure if you love her?" I questioned again.

"I love her, but I don't know if I love her enough."

Our main course arrived and we were gratefully distracted for a few minutes, as we salivated over the smell of freshly-cooked steak.

"So can I ask, did you buy the apartment in France because you wanted space?"

"You are very intuitive, Alana. I guess I did. She's got a job over there that she's going back to but we plan to see each other in holidays and at weekends sometimes."

"So effectively, you've bought HER an apartment." The puzzle was complete.

"Well, I've started to realise that I've got myself into one big mess. But then, some days I think I can make it work."

I dug into my steak and pondered on his situation. It was a tricky one.

"So, does your lady know you are having dinner with me tonight?" I asked, already knowing the answer.

"No." He took another sip of wine.

"And why are you having dinner with me tonight?" I wasn't sure where my bravery and directness were coming from. I sounded like an assertive, wise woman but surely that wasn't me!

"I guess it's not fair on you, Alana. I should have told you the situation but I just had to see if it was still there. And it is. I don't have 'this' with Jemille."

My goodness, she even had a beautiful name!

"What do you mean 'this'?" I was now intrigued and my heart started to beat faster.

"I don't have 'this'. When I'm with you, everything just flows, it's easy, it's natural, it's special. You are special."

It was my turn to re-arrange the placemat and reach for my wine glass. The waitress seemed to intuitively know when to bring the next course, as I was delighted to see my Warm Fudge Sundae appear before me. I could feel his eyes on me.

"I shouldn't have asked you here, Alana, I'm sorry." I could hear the genuine remorse in his voice.

"Forget that thought straight away! Look at this Warm Fudge Sundae! You really want to deny me this?!" I had lightened the mood and his relief was evident in the warm and, dare I say it, loving look he gave me.

"But let's get one thing perfectly clear. I'm here as a friend, chatting through your relationship issues; nothing more. I am sure as hell never being 'the other woman'."

He laughed and I laughed and we clinked our glasses together.
"I'll drink to that", he said, "Alana you are one amazing woman, you know."
And that night I did feel quite amazing. Even though the situation was far from ideal, I felt that Ben had trusted me with his heart's problems. It was a pretty big deal.

Never underestimate correct analysis of photos on Facebook.

CHAPTER 45

August

Facebook messages to'd and fro'd after that night. They flowed naturally, as the conversation had always done with us. I was aware, very aware, of keeping the subjects completely legitimate and light, as a friend should but there was an underlying special tone to all of the messages sent from both sides.

The chatter was mostly to do with work and social lives but there was an uneasy silence about Jemille. I had asked the question "So, any solutions on the love life?" but that had resulted in a particularly long gap between responses and I knew why. He was avoiding the question.

I loved the regular contact. The connection we had seemed to have strengthened but one evening, I questioned my motives. In fact, I questioned my motives every time I received a message because my heart skipped and my face involuntarily smiled. My ego shot upwards and outwards and I felt like a better person; a more valid person; someone worth liking. Here was this man, in the Premier League, emailing me. I must be worth talking to. When I walked, my head was up and my confidence was at an all time high.

But why? Ben was not my boyfriend. In fact, he was not available to be my boyfriend. So why did his messages fill me with such joy and hope? I answered my own question; there was hope. The words he had spoken over steak, "it is special; you are special", reverberated around my brain. They watered the growing seed in my mind, that he was 'The One'. Inside, there was no doubt. We would end up together eventually. I just had to be patient. He had got himself into a mess, as I had many times, but he would set himself free and one day, we would just put together the pieces of our puzzle and it would all make sense.

Every time I realised I was having 'The One' dream again, I stopped myself. I was sounding delusional. All this was just two friends chattering about work and everyday life. Then, on the last day of August...

"Alana, will you have dinner with me?"
My gut reaction was "yes". Unsurprisingly!

All through the joy of connecting with Ben, there was a background battle in my life that he knew nothing about. In fact, only my parents and Frankie knew about Sarah Parker.

Ben was a welcome distraction to counteract the difficult process of my Tuesday afternoons. It had been three months since I had first met Sarah. We had developed a very effective working relationship. I talked, she listened, she probed, I answered and in every 45 minute session, without fail, progress was made, sometimes with many tissues, sometimes not so many. I no longer feared or dreaded Tuesdays but I always knew I would feel drained afterwards. I had come to accept that as part of the process. I was digging deep into my difficult past. It surprised me how many traumatic events had happened during a relatively short marriage of 3 years. When I analysed it, I started to feel true compassion for young Alana.

She had lived with an alcoholic, who regularly drank her weekly wages in one binge. He had stolen her personal possessions and sold them to provide money for drink. He had stripped her of any confidence that once existed by blaming her for his need for drink, manipulating every situation to be her fault. He had made enough threats for her to doubt hers and Jesse's safety in their own home. He had controlled her every move, suppressed every dream and desire she ever had and dismissed her needs as selfish. The drunken times were seemingly never ending. Hospital visits for his injuries during cider-fuelled brawls or overdoses, days of him going 'missing' as he'd got so intoxicated he couldn't remember where he lived and the continuous verbal abuse thrown at Young Alana on a daily basis made her feel worthless. Alcohol was always number one on his priority list and she would sit alone at night dreading the drama that would unfold when he returned from the pub.

Then, between the traumas, dramas and devastation there would be the episodes of remorse, new starts and hopeful moments where she would see the potential in the man she had married, the father of her children. There would be tiny little sparks of hope that would be enough for her to continue, until the next bombshell would fall and destroy all normality and trample on her broken heart again.

The momentous day finally came when I accepted the fact that it was not just 'Young Alana' that all this had happened to. It was me. We were the same person. That's when the tears really fell.

Never underestimate grieving for yourself.

CHAPTER 46

Dinner

The 'Dinner' night came around quickly. For obvious reasons, it was not a 'date' but I seemed to have undertaken exactly the same pre-date rituals of exfoliating and moisturising with the slightly more luxurious products I owned. It had taken me an age to come up with the perfect outfit from my uninspiring collection of clothes and I had frantically been texting Frankie beforehand to get her reassurance. She was slightly more sceptical this time and said:

"He better not be messing you around, Sis, or he'll have me to deal with". I didn't doubt for one second that she'd bop him on the nose if need be.

Also, I was a little more sceptical with myself and heard a similar ringing in my mind, "Don't let him mess you about", but I was feeling far too excited to let that voice be a dampener on the evening.

We'd agreed to meet half-way, in distance that is, and so we arranged to meet in a town I'd never visited. Ben had previously worked there and so he said he knew a few nice eating places. As I pulled into the car park, I saw his cool, black Audi sitting there, with a space just for me next to it. Ben spotted me and gestured over. I had a feeling that this was going to be a wonderful evening. My heart felt happy already, my mind was excited and my body felt alive.

"Alana, so good to see you." He kissed me once for a long peck on the cheek. Mmm, interesting; back to one kiss. This was promising.

"So good to see you, too!" I noticed he was wearing a trendy jacket, "Nice jacket!" I said. He laughed and appreciated the compliment and off we went.

Conversation started and that was it. Ben suggested we travel in his car to a nice gastro pub just up the road. I agreed that the plan sounded perfect. We chatted as he drove and I felt a million dollars. I was being driven in a lovely car by a lovely man. We were both wearing sunglasses to shade our eyes from the evening sun and I thought we looked like the perfect couple.

Damn it. I was not doing a good job of going out for dinner with a friend. I was definitely on a date in my mind. Why did this man set my heart alight? As if he answered the question, he turned to smile at me.

"It's so good to see you."

That was the second time he'd said that. We had been driving for what seemed like a mile when Ben became a little quiet and started looking hesitantly from right to left.

"Um, is everything OK?" I asked.

"Well, the gastro pub seems to have vanished from the face of the earth!"

I laughed. We both laughed.

"Never mind, there is a nice Indian restaurant just a little further up, if that's OK?"

"Of course. That sounds lovely."

We talked about work, the girls, his nieces and nephews and then he pulled into 'The Raj'.

Ben's face dropped. "It looks a little...dark", I said. I could feel Ben's dismay.

"Oh, no! It's closed down!" He looked embarrassed and put his handsome head on the steering wheel. "I'm so sorry, Alana", I should have done more research and booked somewhere. I just assumed these places would still be here!"

"How long ago did you work here?" I asked, as the Raj looked pretty derelict and haunted.

"Mmm, now I come to think of it, I haven't been here for 10 years!"

I laughed and rested my hand on his leg instinctively. "Don't worry, we'll find somewhere. Maybe, if you keep driving up this road?"

I could see that my hand on his leg had stirred something inside of him as he looked across at me in that lustful way I had seen before. I removed my hand and placed it back on my own leg.

Ben shook his head. "Well sack the date planner! Ok, let's keep driving."

I inhaled the last sentence into my brain. 'Date planner', 'Date planner?' 'Date planner!!!!' So, this was not dinner. This was a date? On the outside, I appeared cool. On the inside, I was not; I was all over the place. Did this mean he was now single, as I had clearly stated that I would not be 'the other woman'? Maybe this changed everything.

After a couple of miles, we spotted a place; a family pub which looked a bit in need of a renovation, with a few letters missing from the sign.

"Well, the lights are on at least!" I said, with a cheeky smile.
He laughed and shook his head. "This was not the sort of place I wanted to take you to, Alana." He looked genuinely disappointed.

"Well, I am predicting they have a table and chairs and they sell food and drink. That's all we need."
He smiled across at me again:

Smiles Tally: lllll lllll 1

We entered the pub, which was quite busy.

"You see, it can't be that bad, it's not deserted", I said positively. At that point, a screaming 3-year-old ran past us, quickly followed by a screaming mother. "Get back 'ere, you little…"

My eyebrows raised and Ben and I simultaneously looked at each other. He shook his head with a sad, puppy dog look on his face and I looked sympathetically at his pain.

"Look, why don't we have one drink in here and then we can decide what to do", I said.

"Good plan." He ordered the drinks and I found a quiet area around the corner with a fireplace and some cosy lighting.

"See, it's not so bad", I said, gesturing to the private area I had found." Ben looked relieved as he sat down.

"Yes, this is a bit better", he smiled.

And then we heard the testing of a microphone; a loud microphone. "Testing; 1, 2, 3. Testing; 1, 2, 3."

My J20 involuntarily spluttered out of my mouth, as I let out an almighty laugh.

Ben's hands covered his eyes. "You've got to be joking!"

I looked on the table to see a leaflet advertising 'Open Mic Night'. I picked it up and turned it around to show Ben. "What a treat we have in store?"

"I don't believe it", Ben said, half laughing, half crying. "I think someone is trying to tell me something. Maybe, I shouldn't have taken you out."

I clocked it straight away; guilt. "Mmm, well that all depends on whether you should be taking me out.. I'm guessing that you shouldn't."

I looked Ben straight in the eyes and he said, "It's complicated." He had a sip of his drink and said, "Alana, I can't talk in this X-Factor Audition! Would you mind if we go?" I sensed that the mood of the evening had changed. My mood had already gone from buoyant to flat in a matter of seconds.

"Of course, come on, let's get out of here before I take the mic!" Ben laughed but I could see a seriousness in his face now, so we headed back to the car with slightly less to say for ourselves. The evening had looked a little like this:

Just Dinner-- Definitely a Date --
Just Dinner-- In fact, no Dinner –
A big mess.

We drove back the way we came and I couldn't help thinking that this whole situation reflected our ongoing, confused relationship. We went forwards; it didn't go quite right; we ended up back where we started. There was a lengthy, uncomfortable silence in the car, as I entered a sad room in my head, when realisation hit that, yet again, I had let myself into this vulnerable situation. I'd let him in again but why? Because he was clearly going to tell me, any second now, that he was still confused about Jemille and that he shouldn't have taken me out. I had an urge to get out of the car and be stranded on the side of the road rather than hear the words. But it was too late.

"I'm so sorry, Alana. I wanted tonight to be perfect but I was in denial. It can't be perfect because I am still officially in a relationship in the eyes of the world. For me, it's over but I've not yet ended it properly. I think tonight has made me realise I'm in the wrong."

I took a deep breath and then...there it was; the disappointment, again. The hope dashed and squashed; another blow to the soul, deep inside, where no-one could see. The flower that had grown in my mind chopped down and left on the ground; the weather changing quickly, that big dark cloud in the distance swept into view and all this from just those few words from the man I loved; from 'The One'.

Never underestimate hearing the words you don't want to hear.

CHAPTER 47

Car Park Therapy

I sometimes wished I was a brasher kind of person; someone who would have stormed off in that situation and vowed never to see him again and stuck to it. In that moment, I wished I could have done that. My caring, somewhat ridiculous heart could only now see the hurt in Ben's eyes. My compassionate soul put to one side its own confused, unbalanced emotions and put his to the forefront.

As we drove back towards the car park, where the evening had started with such ease and fluidity, I decided to break the silence.

"It's OK, you know, I'm quite experienced in dates going disastrously wrong." It was a joke to clear the air but it had an element of truth to it. Ben managed a little laugh.

"You are always so positive, Alana; it's a great quality. I wish I could always see the bright side. I'm just not seeing one at the moment."

We parked up, next to my rust bucket car. I really had to save for an upgrade. "I can think of a bright side for you."

"Oh, yes, what's that?" Ben looked over at me but I looked out of the window to avoid his gaze.

"You don't have to drive that every day! The roof leaks in the rain; sometimes I have to sit in a giant puddle on the driver's seat. The bright side is that you get to drive this little beauty."

Ben nodded and smiled. "Yes. Oh, you've got me there. Things are looking up!" I wondered whether I should just continue with the small talk, the little quips to make him laugh but I felt an overwhelming urge to understand him. When would I ever get this chance again; sat, one to one with the man whom I loved, whom I had thought about incessantly for 7 years, whom I just couldn't get out of my head, Kylie style. This was an important moment. I could feel it. This might be my only chance to understand.

"Ben, look, I didn't come out to dinner tonight thinking we were on a date. As the evening went on, it became apparent it was a date. And now, it's definitely not a date. So, let's forget all that and just be Alana and Ben, sitting next to each other in a car, starving hungry due to lack of good restaurants in this part of Swindon. It's 10pm, what do you want to get off your chest?"

"Alana, I'm not good at talking about things like this. I'm not good at saying how I feel. I'm not even good at knowing how I feel. I just know I feel guilty; guilty I've ruined your night; guilty I asked you for dinner; guilty for betraying Jemille. I plead guilty."

"So, what's the sentence for that charge, then?" I asked.

"Unhappiness, Alana. The only time I'm really happy is..." He stopped himself and looked out of the driver's window into the distance.

"Is when, Ben?"

"I think you know, Alana." Ben looked at me with a serious face but my intuition was faltering. I didn't know anything. Everything felt like a big blur.

"The only time I'm really happy is when I'm with you. I don't know what it is, but it's been there since we first met. It's always there. Even when you are nowhere to be seen, you live here." Ben touched the middle of his forehead with his finger. "You live here, in my head."

I listened to his words and could not quite believe it. That was exactly how I had felt for 7 years.

"Well, you live in my head, too, Ben. You live here as well." I put my hand on my heart and inwardly groaned at how lovey-dovey it sounded. But it was true. I couldn't deny it but why did I have to say it out loud?

"Alana, I'm sad a lot of the time and I don't even know why but when I'm with you, things feel so good. It's just when I start thinking too much, I just can't see us together."

There it was again, that big, fat right hook. I wasn't good enough for him. He wanted someone who hadn't got children, who hadn't already been divorced at 21 and who didn't drive a clapped out old banger. He wanted me but without all those things. An impossible dream.

"So, you are in love with me but you don't want to be." I summarised the conversation with clarity.

"It's not that I don't want to be. It's just in my life there are pressures; pressures to be a certain way, love a certain way, marry a certain way. I'm trapped in this life, full of pressures and feel guilt that I want something outside of it."

I knew that when I analysed the conversation at length in my head for days, I would be able to feel the positives. Ben was practically admitting his undying love for me but he gave it with one hand and snatched it away with the other.

"So, Jemille fits the criteria, does she; the 'right' kind of woman with the 'right' background and the 'right' prospects?"

"I can't talk about Jemille, Alana."

Suddenly, my mood changed from compassion to utter annoyance. "I think Jemille has everything to do with this", I said firmly. "Quite honestly, Ben, you are not being fair to either of us."

I could hear the frustration in my voice but getting angry would not solve anything. I tried a different angle. "I'm trying to understand, Ben. Where is this pressure coming from?"

"My whole life, Alana; my whole life, I've had a pressure to live up to the expectation of my family, to continue the Rutherford name with pride; to follow in my father's footsteps, to go to the right school, the right university and, ultimately, marry the right woman." I knew he was opening up to me and my frustration vanished into thin air.

"Ever since we met, I've had this other path in my head; this other life I could be leading, and whenever we've met, it comes alive but it's not my real life."

I related to his words. I, too, lived two lives; one real life, which seemed to be a struggle, with those dark clouds hovering, and then the alternative one, a vision of love and happy-ever-after with 'The One', Ben Rutherford.

"I've tried to ignore it, Alana. I've tried pushing you away. I've tried just being friends. I've tried everything over the years but no matter what, you are always there, being lovely Alana, and I don't know what to do."

I took in what he said. Perhaps, I understood him better than anyone because I was in the exact same position, the only difference being I was all for the relationship and he was all against it. I was the defence and he was the prosecution.

"Ben, I am trying to understand the pressures you are under and I'm putting my feelings to one side. Even if you take what we have out of the equation, you still have to deal with the situation with Jemille. You are being a total ostrich about that." I looked at him, raised my eyebrows and waited for his response.

"I know. It's what I'm best at; burying my head in the sand."

"But, it's doing you no good. I bet you are not sleeping well." Ben looked at me again. I looked right back at him. He smiled right into my eyes with that warmth I craved for.

"Even though I've ruined the evening, you are still caring about me. You are an amazing woman, Alana."

"And you are a frustrating man, Ben Rutherford. Why did I have to fall in love with you? Why did I fall in love with someone I can't have?" I shook my head and smiled. "By the way, you haven't ruined the evening. In fact, sitting here with you in your car is the closest I've ever felt to you. I know it's not ideal and I know that we shouldn't be here because of Jemille, but I could quite literally stay here all night."

It was true. It wasn't what you would imagine a perfect date to be but I felt undeniably close to him.

"Do you know that you are the only person I've talked to about how I feel? I never talk about how I feel. I think, in the world I live in, feeling is not encouraged. You just get on with it and rise up the social ladder with your achievements."

We talked and talked and talked; mostly about him but also about my marriage and how it had changed the course of my life and left behind my own personal struggles to overcome. We listened to each other, with great care and without judgement. We were just two 'in-love' humans on the same wavelength, yearning to be understood, wanting to find our happiness and not wanting the moment to end.

I was aware, in the back of my mind, that I would have to get home at some point. I could not stay out all night, as the girls would not know where I was in the morning and I had not told Mum and Dad I was staying out. I glanced at the car clock. 3.07am. Ben caught my glance and looked at the time, too.

"I don't want you to go, Alana. Everything makes sense when I'm talking to you." He looked straight into my eyes again.

"That's because I talk a lot of sense! To be honest, I don't want to go either, but I have to."

And then it happened. He reached out and took my hand

"I know what I have to do. I will tell Jemille. I have to end it. You are right. Burying my head in the sand is doing me no good." He pulled on my hand until we were inches away from each other. He looked deep into my eyes and he kissed me. He pulled away gently and said, "Alana, will you come to my belated birthday party in October? I would really like you to be there."
He had just kissed my soul. How could I say 'no'?

Two souls, here, in a moment
Eyes locked, lost in a gaze
True love, here, in a moment
Hearts warmed, lost in a daze
For I loved, here, in this moment
Mind wild, lost in a craze
For I loved you, in this moment
As I will, for all of my days

Never underestimate car park therapy.

CHAPTER 48

Pinot Therapy

Frankie carried the Pinots over to the table. It was time for a full update. I had been in a bubble ever since the no-date/date/no-date/car park therapy night the previous week. Every known emotion had travelled through me. But these were the main three:

Happiness –Confusion –Hurt –Happiness – Confusion – Hurt.

In fact, it was less of a flow chart and more of a vicious circle:

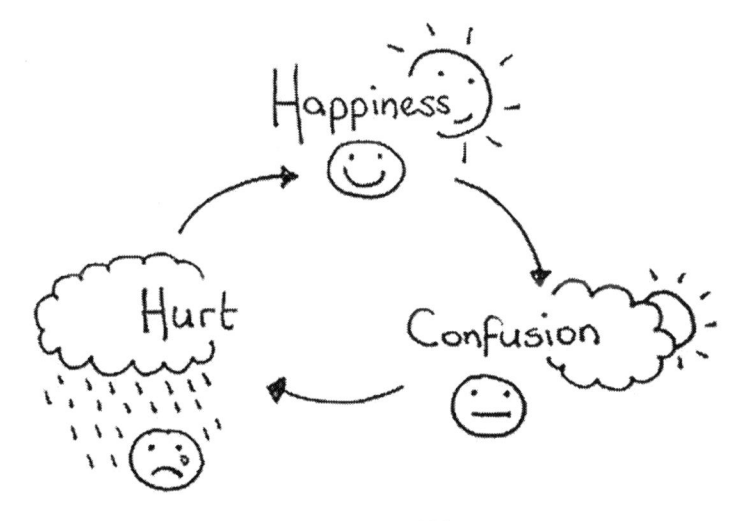

Flow charts usually move situations forwards. That was certainly not the case. I was definitely living in a vicious circle. I relayed to Frankie the entire evening in as short a synopsis as I could manage. She was an amazing listener. At the end of the story, she picked up her glass and said, "Well, it's only a matter of time until I buy my hat. He obviously loves you, Alana, and I think he will come to his senses eventually. Sounds like he may already have!"

I smiled with happiness but then I remembered "But what about Jemille?"

"Well, he's asked you to his birthday party in 2 months. I reckon he is planning to break up with Jemille. Why else would he ask you to the party?"

It had been a theory that I had thought most likely too. He had seemed quite set on this when he kissed me.

"But even if he does break up with Jemille, what about all the other reasons he has for not being with me?"

"I think he's already realised you are the best thing to ever happen to him. I think he will come to his senses, Sis. And if he doesn't, he needs a bop on the head."

Our conversation had calmed me down. I guessed I would just have to wait and see what happened. In the meantime, I would enjoy a night of friendship with Frankie. The rest of the girls were due to meet up later for dancing. That would take my mind off things.
It did, until 11.30pm, when I checked my phone. New email message:

"Subject: Ben's Birthday Bash

Dear All,

I would be delighted if you could join me to celebrate the big 40 on October 9th 2008.
Dress code: Oscar Night. Bring your dancing shoes.

RSVP

Ben x"

I looked at the top of the email at the list of recipients. I looked for her name; I looked for a French email; I looked for anything French. Nothing. There were a lot of names; a mix of men and women. I wondered who these people were and what they meant to him. Then there was my name. He wanted me at his birthday party, to meet all these people. I would be there.

I showed Frankie the email. She looked at me, grabbed me to the dance floor and said, "I did see a nice hat the other day!"

Never underestimate a vicious circle.

CHAPTER 49

DJ Alana

In the two months that passed, life became a little better. The Tuesday counselling sessions had started to transform my mind from a muddled, untidy, overgrown, entangled garden into a somewhat more respectable place. I felt I had dug down deep to unearth the deepest rooted hurt of the married years. It had not been an easy process but facing it head on in that little room, with Sarah Parker, had brought a new respect for myself. It was a brave step.

A knock-on effect of that was having a new energy to look to the future, which had felt like a scary place before. I had lost all faith in having dreams, only for them to be dashed and broken into tiny pieces by other people. Before I was married, I had been a dreamer. One of those dreams had been to be happy ever after with my husband. Later, I had come to the conclusion that dreaming was dangerous because I had clung onto that thought for a long time: "I can't leave him because I need to make this dream work. This is what I want. I must work at it and try everything. I must not give up on it."

I would say that to myself on the darkest days. The days I was bullied; the days I would be told I was boring and frigid by a drunken, slurring, horrible man; the days I ached to be happy; the days I was threatened in my own home, the days I was stolen from. There was no getting away from it. That dream had taken me to dark places. It had started well but it had ended very badly. The dream had kept me hostage and tied me up in knots. It was no wonder I had become wary of dreams.

The future also scared me because I would never have predicted my life to have worked out the way it had. I had been planning to go to university, become a success in something and enjoy life. I had not predicted that I would be married to and divorced from an alcoholic. That had not been my dream.

Whenever I thought like that, I felt a wave of love for my beautiful girls, for without that dream, I would not have had those two beating hearts in my life and the pride and happiness they brought to me daily.

The single, most important thing I learned in counselling was acceptance; acceptance that bad things had happened; acceptance that I'd been broken into tiny pieces, acceptance that I had 2 wonderful girls to take forward with me into the better life I wanted.

So, as I dug up and threw out some of those old, painful times, I realised that my garden was much clearer. It was refreshing.
I was still wary of making any kind of plans or dreaming too big because I didn't believe it had much benefit. I had come across my 'I want' list a few days before and I still looked at it sceptically.
I had achieved (1) = I had great relationships with the girls and family; I had achieved (2) - maintained sistership with Frankie; I had achieved (3) - the drama groups were going well; (4) - I hadn't achieved 4 - the holiday, as money was still tight; (5) was all up in the air (relationship with a great man), however, I did now own a couple

of pairs of really nice heels. (6) – I needed to find a good book; (7) – Write a book. Pah. I had completed two A4 journals of my thoughts but becoming an author was never going to happen. (8) – Frankie and I were closer to the spa. We'd decided which one we'd like to go to but we still hadn't been; (9) – be happy. Mmm, I'd had glimpses of the stuff. The girls brought me the most happiness and, of course, THAT kiss and THAT date/non-date but it was not happy in the true sense; (10) – find myself. I looked at this one for a while and realised that I had found myself. I was definitely not who I wanted to be yet; I was not even close, but the voice in my head was mine. That, in itself, was reassuring. Temporary insanity had subsided.

During those two months, there had also been a few interactions with Ben. They were light-hearted and friendly; perhaps over-friendly at times, but they brought big smiles to my face. The most relevant one to talk about was this one:

"Dearest Alana,

I'm wondering if I can ask you a favour. Out of all my friends, I believe you to be the most likely to be able to put together a brilliant party playlist for my birthday. Is this possible? My one request is 'Billie Jean'– it's a classic, don't you think? I'm thinking a mix of old and new. Would you like the challenge? If not, I totally understand, as you already have a million and one things to do with your time.
I really can't wait to see you.

Ben xx"

"I really can't wait to see you." It made my insides melt and my heart beat faster and my mind wander to the future event. I really had to decide on an outfit.

I accepted the DJ challenge with both hands and perhaps put slightly more thought into it than was necessary. I put aside work stuff to listen to tracks and found myself dancing around the room imagining dancing with Ben and showing off my best moves. The dreams were enjoyable and uplifting and life felt, dare I say it, exciting.

I continued to write in my journal and amazingly managed to fill numerous pages of A4 about Ben's emails, the party invite, the playlist request. I analysed every word and when I re-read the entries, I could practically feel the love oozing out of the pages.

Ben would undoubtedly have champagne. He was the champagne of all men in my eyes. Most other men were ciders or beers – after too much you just feel ill. Some men were slightly better. I'd had a few fine wines but they did not compare to Ben. Ben was champagne because there was always an element of quality in every single encounter, bubbles of excitement came to my surface and I savoured every single moment. The champagne was offered little and often and I always felt like the person I should be when drinking it in. I stood a bit taller, held my glass more confidently and raised my topic of conversation.

I think, deep down, if I admitted it to myself, perhaps I also dreamed a little of Ben walking me back to the hotel after the party. Perhaps he would want to say goodbye and perhaps we would share a lift up to my room and perhaps...well for someone who did not rate dreaming as a good idea, the dreams were coming thick and fast. 3 days and counting. Wardrobe crisis!

Never underestimate allowing yourself to dream again.

CHAPTER 50

Prepared

On the day of the party, I sorted the girls' dinner and clothes for the next day. I gave them both big cuddles and left them playing in the garden, in the sunshine, with their beloved Nana.

"Have a great time, Mummy", Jesse called out.

"I will", I promised. I had no doubt I would have a great time. I grabbed my overnight bag, which sounded posh but, in fact, was a Tesco carrier, with a pair of PJs, my old make-up bag, which needed sorting out, my perfume and underwear, my heeled shoes and change of clothes for the next day.

I walked out to the car and hooked my dress onto the back seat hanger. I checked my reflection in the rear view mirror. My eyes looked sparkly. That was a good start.

The journey was about a two-hour drive. I inserted the 'Party' CD into the car stereo and proceeded to float off in my half dream/half reality state all the way there. I smiled at other drivers, I was generous at give way points and I sang my little heart out. I was positively happy and wondered when I had last felt like that. I couldn't remember; maybe, to a point, in that dark and deserted car park.

I pulled up at the hotel and smiled again. It was my home for the night. I had left enough time to have a shower and freshen up before the party and I could feel myself transforming from being a Mum to being Alana. Motherhood was a funny thing; you were always on duty, always thinking and analysing your children's moods, happiness, minor events, major events, food intake, sugar intake, hydration levels, social situations, sleep patterns and general well-being. It was only when you were actually physically distanced from them that the mind calmed slightly and allowed a little bit of time to think about yourself. It was not something I did often enough, but being the only parent in the equation, it was just not possible. So, when it did happen, I appreciated and relished the 'Me' time.

I soon realised I was in one of those annoying, nervous moods when I worked very inefficiently. I started to run the shower, then decided instead to check my outfit was OK, then went back to the shower, only to realise I hadn't taken my wash bag into the bathroom with me. I was in the shower a little longer than I should have been and then found myself rushing to dry my hair and slap on a little bit of make-up.

I sat at the dressing table and smiled into the mirror. I didn't look too bad. It was a relief. I had decided to be Angelina Jolie for the night. Ben had indicated that he was going as Brad Pitt, so it was the obvious choice. I had recycled a black dress, the only black dress I possessed. It had been a bargain buy and looked more expensive than it was. It had straps and a slit to half-way up the thigh. I glanced at the slit in the mirror and, for a second, thought that it was perhaps a little too risqué. I put my little black shrug on, although I didn't think I would need it, as it was a mild evening and I could feel my nerves raising the temperature in my cheeks. I put on my black heels and checked my purse and phone. One new message:

FRANKIE – ALANA   "Keep me posted!!!"

I laughed. Frankie always knew when to send the right message. I suddenly felt extremely nervous. I was going to a party where I didn't know a soul, apart from Ben. Jenna and Michael were away in Mexico and I had never been in Ben's social circle before. I also remembered that Ben's social circle would probably be very different from mine. Most of his friends would be Oxford University graduates, private school buddies, or high-level barristers and politicians.

I sat down on the bed. What was I doing? Why was I here? I also had a flash of concern that Ben had not mentioned anything about Jemille for over 2 months. I had concluded that he wouldn't have invited me if he was still with her, but I had not had confirmation of that. How would I walk into a room of strangers? How would I make conversation with them? I considered staying on the bed and curling up into a ball but then I thought about Ben. He was the reason I had driven here. He was the reason I had spent the last 2 hours trying to look presentable. He was the reason I'd been looking forward to this night for 2 months. His words rang in my ears:

"I'm so glad you can make it. It wouldn't be the same without you, Alana."

I had to go. I just had to get over the moment of stage fright. I would have to act my way out of this worrying burst of self-doubt. What would Angelina Jolie do in my position? She'd do a cartwheel, high kick someone and get on with it without a hair out of place. I picked up my hotel key and left the room with a firm self-talking to: "Get a grip, Alana. I mean Angelina."

Never underestimate overcoming stage fright.

CHAPTER 51

The Big Entrance

I'd love to say I glided elegantly down the road towards the party venue but to my dismay, one shoe felt slightly on the big side and so it dragged along behind me, somewhat annoyingly.

I found a way of clenching my toes together and tensing my foot so that I would look less awkward when making my entrance. I could see the place up ahead. Ben had found an exclusive bar and would be the sole hirer of the night. There were men in tuxedos entering the building and a couple of glamorous looking ladies. Did I look glamorous enough? I could feel the slit of the dress rising up as I walked and the word 'tart' popped into my head. Damn, I was not aiming for 'tart'. I was aiming for 'sophisticated'. My cheeks still felt flushed and I tried to breathe a little slower.

Before I knew it, I was right outside the door. Two handsome men stood before me and let me in. The shorter of the two glanced around and caught my eye. I smiled happily, my party excitement finally hitting my face.

"Hello!", the man smiled back with a twinkle in his eye. "After you", as he held the door open. I found myself automatically put a little strut into my walk, as a statement of confidence, and said a warm "thank you" to Mr Twinkly Eyes.

The room was already busy and the lights were dimmed, so I could only see outlines of smartly dressed people. The noise of clinking glasses and laughter filled the air and I scanned the room for Ben. My radar captured his voice immediately, as it always did. I was convinced he emitted a different frequency to all other humans.

I looked in his direction and perhaps his radar was as attuned as mine, as he looked over at exactly the same time. Our eyes met and a smile grew on my face as he simultaneously smiled back, made his excuses to his friends and walked over. I saw him clock the dress and I looked away, surveying the room, knowing his eyes were still on me. Then he was right there in front of me.

"Alana, you look stunning." He kissed me on the cheek and I smelt his aftershave, making me breathe deeply into his neck.

"Don't you mean Angelina?" I smiled and raised an eyebrow. I caught a glimpse of something in his eyes before he smiled but I couldn't quite read it. Was it panic; or surprise; or something else? Had I been too daring with my choice? He was Brad Pitt after all. I was making a bold statement by being Angelina. The fleeting moment of doubt was soon forgotten.

"Alana, or Angelina, whoever you are, I'm very glad you could make it. Let me get you a drink." I could feel his arm rest on my back as he ushered me towards the bar. The 2-hour drive had been worth it for that moment alone.

At the bar, we chatted while the bartender poured my wine. I couldn't take my eyes off Ben and it seemed mutual. Suddenly, a man and a woman appeared beside us, smiling at Ben mischievously. I again clocked this look and didn't quite understand it but perhaps, there was a private joke that I was unaware of. After all, I did not know these people. It was a harsh reminder; I did not know anyone!

" Cameron, Victoria, I'd like you to meet Alana." We shook hands warmly and I liked Victoria instantly. She had a sparkle to her.
I caught Victoria give Ben an approving smile; it was very brief and it was covered up well but my radar was on high alert and I was missing nothing.

"Oh, before I forget..DJ Alana saves the day!" I fished out the Party CD from my bag and handed it to Ben.

"Brilliant! I'll go and get them to put it on the sound system." Ben rushed off and I was left with my two new favourite strangers. Cameron was already engaged in conversation with another good-looking man. Victoria, however, seemed to be smiling at me as if she'd known me for years.

"So, you are Alana", she exclaimed. "I can absolutely see why Ben wanted us to meet you. You are beautiful." It was never a compliment I believed but coming from this complete stranger of a woman, it made me smile.

"Ben wanted you to meet me?" I registered the news out loud.

"Well, he was at our house for dinner last week and he said that there was someone special coming to the party. He mentioned your name. He's often mentioned your name over the years."
My heart skipped and I imagined Frankie would have said the same to Ben. Victoria continued..."I just saw the two of you talking at the bar. I watched for a minute and I said to Cameron, 'That's Alana. She is the one'."

I took a big sip of wine and drank in her words. A huge wave of happiness swept over me and my heart and soul clapped excitedly inside. Ben had spoken to his best friends about me. I had heard Ben speak about Cam and Vic many times. In fact, I felt like I knew Victoria very well but I was not sure if that was because of the stories I had heard from Ben or whether it was simply her overwhelmingly warm personality that made me feel at instant ease.

"So, Alana, tell me, do you love him?" I could not believe I was having this conversation. I had only been at the party for 10 minutes and I had already felt so many emotions. The current one was openness.

I looked over at the back of Ben's head. He was talking to the bar staff about the CD. The back of his head was as attractive as the front; it had been what I couldn't take my eyes off at the very first meeting. I looked at Victoria and nodded slowly.

"I've been in love with Ben Rutherford for a hundred years, I think. Well, it feels like that." A pang of pain leapt across my chest as I remembered the sequence of events; the unreplied-to letter, the rejection, the dates, the non-date, the rejection, the chats, the silence, the rejection, the French woman, the car park, the confusion.

However, in that very moment, all I could feel was relief; relief that perhaps Ben Rutherford was feeling the same as me. Perhaps, it was all going to work out after all. Being brave and coming to a party full of strangers was the best thing I could have done.

How quickly emotions can change.

Never underestimate the words of strangers.

CHAPTER 52

The Big Entrance II

It could not have been a more timely entrance for dramatic effect. I had just admitted my true love to one of Ben's best friends when I noticed a tall, beautiful woman enter the room. She was accompanied by a slightly shorter but equally beautiful woman who was very similar in looks; perhaps sisters. It took me only a few awful seconds to realise it was Jemille.

I had always seemed to have the intuitive power to survey a room and I glanced across at Ben, who had also just noticed the newcomers. His face dropped slightly but he covered it well with a flustered walk to greet them. I watched carefully...they kissed briefly on the lips. On the lips!

I became aware that I was deadly silent and had cut short my wonderful chat with Victoria about the love of my life. I turned my head slightly to look at Victoria's reaction. I knew instantly that she had read the situation as clearly as me.

"Oh, my darling, let's go to the bar, get another drink, we need to talk."

I silently finished the wine in my glass and followed Victoria. I felt like I had fallen from a high building. My face could not fake a smile, not even a little one and it had become used to faking smiles through the years, covering hard emotions and keeping a brave face for the world, but not right at that moment. Finally, I managed to speak:

"Are they still together?" I glanced behind and saw Ben talking to the two French girls. I quickly re-directed my gaze to the new drink Victoria handed me.

"I thought Ben was sorting it out. I thought he'd planned to end it. Well, put it this way, he planned to...but it's looking increasingly like he didn't go through with it. Oh, he's such a nightmare, Alana. He hates hurting people so ends up not dealing with things but I know you are special to him and I think you are brilliant. I've only known you for 5 minutes and I already know you are right for him. He's just got to sort this mess out with 'The Ice Queen'.

I questioned her, "The Ice Queen?"

"Oh, you haven't met her then? You'd know what I mean. She is beautiful, yes, on the outside, but she is cold, Alana. We tried to get along with her for Ben's sake but she is just very hard work and very manipulative. When Ben talks about Jemille, his eyes are sad; when he talks about you, they light up. That's all you need to know."

I listened to Victoria's words and I took some comfort from them.

"He wanted us to meet you, Alana. He said there was someone coming to the party he wanted us to meet because he thought she might be 'The One' and I agree with him."

Since I had arrived at the party, an hour had passed in time; a momentous hour in many ways. Victoria's words enveloped me; they seeped deep into my soul and a small part of me was dancing on the ceiling with the news that Ben's eyes 'light up' when he talked about me. It was important news; very important.

As my eyes turned again towards Ben, who was still by her side, I could feel my heart bleeding, Leona Lewis style. It was seeping out of an old wound. I felt like I needed to be rushed to an Accident and Emergency Department, away from the party, with an oxygen mask for me to control my breathing. Maybe, they would send me straight to the psychiatric unit, as surely I was now deemed insane for driving 150 miles to be in a room with the man I adored, watching him apparently pretending to adore someone else. No-one called 999 for me. So I had to deal with it. I breathed in deeply; I drank my drink and said to my new favourite person, Victoria, "This round is mine." I wasn't sure if I was talking about the drinks or whether I had virtually stepped into a boxing ring. I suddenly felt a huge amount of fight inside me.

Never underestimate finding your fighting spirit.

CHAPTER 53

Crossroads

I decided to take myself off to the ladies cloakroom; I had consumed 3 glasses of wine and I was in a very sticky situation. I sat down on the toilet seat and put my head in my hands. I did not expect to be in that position. I did not even feel compelled to text Frankie for help. I was too embarrassed. I had come to a party in the hope that Ben Rutherford would kiss me on the lips but he had just kissed his girlfriend on the lips. I only knew, or half knew, two other people in a room full of strangers. It was dire. Why had Ben let me humiliate myself? Surely, he would have known that would happen? That I would end up crying in a toilet cubicle. Surely he saw that coming. To my surprise, no tears had actually fallen. In fact, I think my eyes were still wide with shock at what they had seen. I closed them and settled myself down. I decided that it was time for a good talk with myself. I came round to the thought that I had three options: (1) leave now, go back to the hotel and never contact Ben again; (2) stay there in the cubicle and cry like a baby, feel sorry for myself, leave the party with swollen eyes and mascara running down my face; (3) get out into that party, focus on everybody else in the room, make friends and enjoy the music I had spent hours choosing.

The first 2 options were tempting. They required the least strength and energy but the third option was a fighting one. I had proved, in my life so far, that I was strong. I had battled to survive in circumstances far harder than this. Surely, I could strut out of the toilet and make friends. I was good at making friends. I was a warm person. People often told me that. I was no Ice Queen. Maybe I was a Sun Queen. Forget Angelina Jolie. I had noticed Jemille's hair was slicked back in an Angelina Jolie style and Ben's glance earlier all made sense now. He'd known Jemille was coming as Angelina. It was an embarrassed wince. Well, Angelina was now out of my mind. I was going to avenge the situation. Not by violence or throwing drinks over people's heads, however tempting. This moment was about rising above the situation and not letting it drag me down. I unlocked the cubicle, washed my hands, brushed my hair, sprayed some perfume and smiled at myself in the mirror. I was ready. It was time to work the room.

Never underestimate being a Sun Queen.

CHAPTER 54

Work it

I headed to the bar and ordered another drink. I smiled at the two gentlemen standing next to me and realised it was Mr Twinkly Eyes and his friend from the start of the evening.

"We'll add your drink to our tab; a lovely lady like you shouldn't ever have to buy her own drink." On some days, I could have read that as quite a sexist comment but I was relieved for the compliment and I went with it by flirting with my smile and raising my eyebrows in appreciation.

"Why, thank you, that's very kind", I said, as the barman handed me my drink. He also seemed to have sparkly eyes syndrome and I smiled back for slightly too long. I was definitely working it.

Mr Twinkly eyes obviously wanted to strike up conversation and before long, we were chatting about how we knew the birthday boy.

"We were at school together. Great days. Haven't seen him for years but he seems to have fallen on his feet!" He nodded towards Ben, who was sitting with Jemille and the supposed sister. "So, how do you know Ben?"

How I wanted to tell him the truth. 'Well, he loves me apparently but he is an Ostrich' but I told him the other truth, "We're friends of friends. Ben's brother is married to a good friend of mine."

"So, is your other half not here then?" Twinkly Eyes was fishing.

"Oh, there is no other half." No truer words were spoken, especially after the evening's events.

"Well, that is tremendous news for the single men of the world. Sorry, I do not know your name?"

"Alana." He shook my hand and smiled.

I decided it was time to expand my circle of new friends and excused myself from the obviously flirtatious twosome.

I spotted a quieter group of people sitting in a corner. There was one chair available. My new found determination to work the party was in full flow. I approached the table and asked if I could join them. I was welcomed with smiles. I explained that I didn't know anyone at the party and it was all a bit awkward. Before I knew it, the table were laughing at my jokes and seemed happy to have my company. It had transformed from the quiet area to the buzzing area. I had my back to the room but I suddenly felt his presence.

One of the men from my new group of friends called for Ben to join us.

"Hey, Ben, drag yourself away from your beautiful woman. We've hardly seen you." Edward was a funny man, I could tell. I could feel Ben's body right beside me now. I did not give him the satisfaction of looking up at him. Instead, I continued my conversation with Sarah, Edward's wife. She was an interesting woman; a writer and a mother of 3. I could hear his voice run through me. He was acting as well as me, pretending everything was fine and dandy, when how could it be? I took a big sip of wine and then felt a hand on my arm.

"Alana, can I get you a drink?" I turned involuntarily. It was Ben. His eyes looked desperate.

"I'm fine, thank you." I stared long and hard into his eyes. "I think I've had enough." The words had a double meaning and he knew it.

He lowered his voice, "Please, Alana. I have to speak with you."
Just then, a glass rang out: "Speeches!"
His eyes rolled and he looked utterly miserable. Cameron ushered Ben over to the table where there was a cake and presents. The room erupted into birthday song and he blew out the candles and made a rather memorable speech.

"Thank you to each and every one of you for being here tonight. Special thanks to my lovely Mum and Dad for organising this amazing cake and to my friend Cameron for organising the night." I noticed Jemille stand up and look at Ben..."and my girlfriend for making this the best birthday ever", and then he looked at me. I picked up my glass and I walked out of the venue while people applauded his speech and sang "For he's a jolly good fellow..."

Never underestimate knowing when to leave a room.

CHAPTER 55

The Taxi Home

The fresh air hit me hard, just as reality did. I drank the last of the wine in my glass and looked up to the stars. 'What was I doing here?' Just then, the door opened behind me. I glanced round to see the Sparkly Eyed Barman light up a cigarette as he walked over and stood beside me.

"He's a fool", he said to me, "Absolute idiot." I looked across at him,

"Who?"

"The man you're in love with." He took a puff of his cigarette and leant perfectly on the wall. "I'm a people watcher. In my job it's all there is to do and my conclusion is that he's not worth your time."

I breathed in the night air. A few cars whizzed past but other than that, it was very quiet against the loud music blasting from inside; the music I had so lovingly prepared.

"Do you know him?" I asked, inquisitive of his opinionated analysis of the situation.

"Never met him before tonight but I've watched and I've listened and I think you should run. You are in a league of your own. Don't let him bring you down." I looked at him again and saw how his eyes were soft and caring; his white shirt open now at the top and his lean body perfectly formed. He was a fine specimen.

"But you don't know me!" I said, bemused. "You don't know my life, who I am, what I do, what car I drive; how can you possibly know?"

"I know, having watched you from the moment you walked into the bar, because the room stopped and stared. I know from the way you smile openly and move with a sparkle few ever possess. I know from the hurt in your eyes when his girlfriend entered. I know you deserve more than that. The trouble is...you don't know." He took another puff of his cigarette and he smiled. "You've got to know, Alana. You are special."

"How do you even know my name?" I frowned at him. It felt like he was some sort of fairy-godmother.

"I was at the bar when that old guy asked your name, remember?" I did remember; that was Mr Twinkly Eyes. I wouldn't have said he was old but he was compared to the barman.

"So, when did you become so wise?" I asked him, smiling over at him. He had soothed my mood. If he was a fairy-godmother, I liked his disguise.

"Maybe I recognise the signs. Maybe I've been there." He finished his cigarette and said, "If you feel like coming back inside, I'll buy you a drink. That'll confuse him!" and he winked cheekily.

I smiled, eternally grateful to my seventh new friend of the night. It was sobering and heart-warming how complete strangers could be so kind.

The door opened again. This time it was Victoria. She held both my hands and said, "He's an idiot, Alana. I can't understand him and I've just told him that!"

I tallied it up:
    11; two people who thought he was an idiot in the last few minutes.

I shook my head, "I'm the idiot, Victoria." She put her arm around me and squeezed my shoulders.

"Look, Cam and I have got to get back to the babysitters. Do you want to come back to ours for a coffee?" Again, the kindness of new friends amazed me.

"I love you for everything you've said to me this evening. I'm so glad we met, but I'll be fine."

"I hope we meet again when he gets his act together." She kissed me on the cheek and went back inside to find Cameron. I breathed in one more night air breath and re-entered the party room.

There were lots of people on the dance floor now and, in normal circumstances, I would have joined them. Instead, I walked over to the barman, who flashed a big smile. "Good on you, girl", he rooted around for a champagne flute and poured a glass of bubbly.

"Nothing but the best for you, remember?" I went to pay but he said, "On the house. Actually, I'm just adding it to your Lordship's tab. It's the least he can do."

I laughed out loud. In fact, I continued to laugh at Seb's jokes, quips and observations of people and I continued to drink bubbles.

Eventually, the room began to empty and I noticed that Jemille did not look at all happy. In fact, she had not cracked a smile all evening. Ben looked distressed and he glanced over and caught my eye. I looked away quickly back to Seb, who expertly poured me another glass.

Jemille left for the ladies cloakroom and Ben instantly walked over to the bar.

"Alana", he started.

I stopped him in his tracks. I stood up, a little wobbly, from the stool.

"Happy birthday, Ben. I hope you've had a really brilliant night." The sarcasm split the air like a knife.

"Alana..."

I cut him short again. "Just want to say thanks so much for inviting me here to meet your girlfriend."

"Alana, let's not have this conversation now."

I felt an emotion I rarely encountered. Was it rage?

"Oh, no, of course we shouldn't spoil your birthday party. No. I mean, why would you invite me to a party knowing I love you, to meet your girlfriend, who I thought you'd broken up with? No, let's not have that conversation now."

"Alana, you are drunk." Ben frowned.

"Good observation", I said and sat back on the stool.

Jemille appeared back from the cloakroom and left the bar with her sister.

"Alana, how are you getting back to the hotel?" Ben asked, as he slowly and sadly walked to follow Jemille.

"She's got a lift", Seb, my Number One hero spoke up. "I'll make sure she gets back safely."

Ben looked far more distressed than I had ever seen him and he had brought it all on himself. What an idiot.

lll – idiot tallies.

Seb did drop me back to the hotel, in his rust-bucket of a car. I felt quite at home in it.

"I'll never see you again, Alana, but promise me this...want more for yourself. He doesn't deserve you."

I had felt every emotion possible during the last 5 hours but, right that minute, I felt huge gratitude to this charming, intuitive, wise and totally handsome young man. He had saved me from despair and made me laugh through the drama.

I leaned over and kissed him on the lips; a precious kiss that he deserved. He wasn't the man I had imagined kissing for the previous

2 months but he was the man who deserved it. In that moment, I had a huge wave of love for him and, possibly, a huge wave of love for myself.

I thanked him and left the car. I walked to my hotel room and it spun for far too long. It may have been the events of the night but, in all probability, it was Seb's bubbles.

Never underestimate a fairy godmother in a gorgeous disguise.

CHAPTER 56

Breakfast

The sun woke me far too early in the morning. I had been too intoxicated to undress or draw the curtains and I was regretting all of the above. I scrunched up my face and hunted around for my phone. I eventually found it under my pillow.

4 missed calls, Ben Rutherford. I looked at the time of calls: 2am, 3am, 4am, 5am. I frowned at the phone. My heart did not flutter. I checked the time: 8.30am. Breakfast was until 10am and I could feel my hangover stomach craving a full English breakfast. I had to eat before I drove home; it was a must. I jumped in the shower and put on my jeans and a T-shirt, far less Angelina-looking. I was past caring.

I entered the breakfast room bleary-eyed. I filled my plate from the buffet and then heard a familiar voice.

"Alana, darling, come and join us." It was Mr Twinkly Eyes. I was not at all in the mood for company but I could not think quickly enough to divert to a different route. I sat myself down opposite him and his friend.

"Oh, dear, Alana, one too many last night?" It was that obvious.

"Yes you could say that." I mumbled.

"Good night, wasn't it?"

"No, it wasn't actually." I really should have diverted my route. I was not good company.

"Oh, why not darling?"

"Long story." I tucked into my sausage and savoured the calories.

"Well, we're in no rush, are we Neil. What happened?"

"I discovered Ben Rutherford is an idiot." I took another bite of sausage. Neil and Twinkles glanced at each other and looked again at me.

"Ah, that kind of long story!" Neil said, nodding his head.

"I think it's probably best we change the subject", I said pleadingly.

"Of course; the weather is looking great today", Twinkles said, relieved to be steered away from the awkward subject of Ben. I was hoping to never speak of him again. Case closed.

Never underestimate how grumpy one can feel the next morning.

CHAPTER 57

The Long Drive Home

There was a heaviness in the car on the way home; a stark contrast to the drive the previous day, which had been full of hope, excitement, joyful expectation and music.

I could not bear to have music playing. My head was thumping and my heart was glumping. I wanted to wallow in my own self-pity. I wanted to beat myself into a pulp because I had managed to end up in a dire situation, which should only have been possible in movies.

Two trails of thought prevailed and I alternated between the two for the entire journey: A) the words that Victoria had said to me: "He wanted us to meet you." How she talked about Jemille, the Ice Queen; the encouraging words she spoke to me. I hung on this string of hope until the other thought appeared; B) the moment that Jemille walked through the door and he kissed her on the lips.

As I drove along at 70 mph, I felt my heart break yet again; my face frowned with hurt and my head pounded with a dull agony, similar to that which I had experienced when he had written to say I was not 'suitable'.

<u>Humiliation</u>: Synonyms: embarrassment; mortification; shame; indignity; disgrace; discredit.

Informal: blow to one's pride/ego; slap in the face; kick in the teeth.

Humiliation was definitely the emotion at the forefront of every thought. The informal synonyms were the closest descriptions. The blow to my ego, what was left of it, felt severe, like a knock out. The slap in the face was still stinging my cheek and the kick in the teeth was so hard I was surprised that I had any left. There was no doubt that the shocking events of the night, the unexpected entrance and appearance of Jemille had hit me like a tonne of bricks. I had no fight left in me.

Once again, the negative voices swarmed like wasps in my head. 'You'll never be good enough for him'; 'You're not beautiful enough'; 'He doesn't want you'.

I stopped at the services and bought a latte. I sat in the car park and I tried to think of something else. Anything else. But my mood was dejected. My heart was really crying this time. As I sipped my coffee through the hole in the lid, I burnt my tongue. A little tear involuntarily fell down my cheek. I needed my girls.

Never underestimate the little tears.

CHAPTER 58

Snakes and Ladders

A few days passed by and I immersed myself back into everyday life. I concentrated on being a good Mum, arranging more days out for the girls. I played music and I completed 10 Sudoku's. I realised that I had learnt some coping strategies for when I slid down a serpent on the game of snakes and ladders with Ben Rutherford. For that's what it felt like. You never knew what you were going to get when you rolled the dice. Sometimes, you went a few squares forwards, then every so often, a ladder appeared and excitement and joy filled the air. Then, with the next roll of the dice, you landed on the biggest snake of the game and there you were, back at Square One.

I tried desperately to fill every moment of time with something, anything, so that I would not have to listen to those annoying wasps buzzing in my head, reminding me that: a) I was a loser; b) I was humiliated; c) I was crazy; d) I was a desperado. Each wasp gave a nasty sting.

I had turned my phone off, a very rare and essential move. Ben had called 10 times since the party and I couldn't bear to avoid his call again, so I switched it off. I'd messaged Frankie to let her know I was OK. I briefly filled her in and she replied, "I hope you poured a drink over him!" It made me chuckle, as I had been very close to doing that! She knew me well!

Eventually, though, I turned it back on: one new voicemail:
 "Alana, I really don't know what to say but I need to speak with you...please...if you will just call me back...I want to explain."
I listened to his voice. It sounded on the brink of desperate but it hit me, as it always did, deep into my soul. Even when I was so mad with him, even when I didn't want to ever speak to him again, his voice made me close my eyes and breathe deeply. It was completely involuntary. God damn that annoying man!

It was late, the girls had been asleep for a while and I had crawled into my bed. I looked at my phone. What could he possibly be able to explain? He had let me walk into a car crash situation in the full knowledge that I would get hurt. What more proof could I possibly have that he didn't care about me at all?

Yet, there he was, 10 calls later, still attempting to put things right. If he didn't care, he wouldn't call. Against my better judgement, I called him. My heart beat fast and my face felt flushed. I had no idea what I felt or what I was going to say.
He answered straight away. "Alana, thank you for calling me. I feared you would never speak to me again and I would not have blamed you."
 "Well, I haven't decided whether I'm speaking to you yet." I was serious but I could already feel a massive part of the ice in my heart melting.
 "I wanted to tell you personally, not on a text or email, how incredibly sorry I am about what happened. I should not have put you in that position and I wish I could turn back the clock."

Turning back the clock had been my greatest wish for a long time. If

I could have turned back the clock, I would never have written that first letter. It had put me in a vulnerable situation ever since.

"Alana, I've got a lot of thinking to do. I'm not happy and I know I'm not. I know what I've got to do and should have done it ages ago. I'm asking if you will be patient with me; if you can forgive me?"

"Ben, forget the party. Forget me. Focus on yourself. All I want is for you to be happy."

I did not know where the kind and generous words sprang out from. Surely, it wasn't me talking, as I was still hurt, still angry, still humiliated.

"Alana, you are an amazing woman. I do not expect you to wait for me but I want you to know how special you are."

I melted some more and wise Alana, the woman who seemed to have taken over my talking voice, calmly said, "Ben, you know how special you are to me. Now get off this phone and start working on being happy."

"I will, Alana. I'll be in touch. I'm sorry again for everything."

So, the fifty conversations I had planned out in my head, the raging 'how could you do that to me?', the insulting "you are an absolute idiot', the bitter 'I'm never talking to you again' role plays had all been a complete waste of time. Two days of imagining what I would say to make him feel my pain.

I rested my head on the pillow and wondered where generous, kind Alana had popped up from. She was so calm. Why hadn't she wanted to rant and rave at Ben? Then a small voice inside said 'because she loves him and wants him to be happy'.

It was true.

Everything hangs in the balance
A corner turned to nowhere
Nothing in front of me
And nothing near me is real
Yet, everything within my grasp
I intensely feel.
To be thinking, just thinking
Is an impossible place to be
My thoughts are wasted.
The mere anticipation in my mind
Of all that could be -
But what is not yet defined.
The darkness of uncertainty
Relieved only by a flicker of hope
Dreams dance in the shadows
Then falter in the stream of smoke
To think of love and yet always be confined
Is conducive to the most torturous frame of mind.

Never underestimate how many hours are wasted imagining conversations that never happen.

CHAPTER 59

Firm Feet

So, I picked up the pieces of myself again. I noticed that although I had felt pretty shattered to begin with, I had not actually broken into as many pieces as I first thought. It was like I had been hit by a thunderbolt and a heavy downpour but now the storm had cleared, the sky was blue underneath. That horrible looming cloud of glumness and inexplicable heaviness was in my life less frequently. I had been seeing Sarah Parker for well over 10 months. I had not missed a single session. The process had astounded me. The start had been incredibly hard and hurtful. Tears had fallen thick and fast in that big, old house. It was sometimes hard to leave the emotions in the room at the end of the session, so I had made a routine of walking home slowly and analysing what I'd covered in the 45 minutes of therapy.

<u>Therapy:</u> treatment intended to relieve or heal a disorder; a treatment that helps someone feel better, grow stronger etc.

Although it was called counselling, I personally preferred the term therapy. I had healed the open wounds of my marriage, which I had left wide open for so long. Poor young Alana was finally being heard and treated with the correct mental medicine – attention and understanding. I became an expert at looking at the wounds closely, inspecting them, finding out where the pain was, what triggered it and then working on a natural remedy to help the healing.

I began to understand why I had felt so much hurt in relationships. When wounds were still open, it only took a tiny little knock or nudge to feel excruciating pain. I had been so unaware and disconnected from the young Alana that I had no idea that the pain and turmoil was coming from her wounds.

As I made sense of it all and started to piece things together, I found that my feelings of dread for Tuesday afternoons turned into positive anticipation. I would plan my session in advance and come prepared with my internal magnifying glass, like a human scientist wanting to find as many answers as possible.

Sarah Parker became increasingly impressed by the way that I was devoted to my own healing and she said on more than one occasion, "I have never seen anyone work so hard to understand themselves. A lot of people choose a 6-week block, to tell themselves they've had counselling and are back on track. You could have done that Alana but instead, you are still here, working hard 10 months later. You are so intent on understanding yourself. It's remarkable. You have come such a long way in the time I've known you. Do you feel that, too?" Sarah Parker smiled a big smile.

I breathed in the compliment and did not brush it aside. Sarah had helped me save myself from destruction and guided me to find my own path of healing. She had given me a safe place to dissect my mind and helped to give me the tools I needed to cope. Her words of praise rang like happy bells in my ears. I felt a wonderful emotion inside: pride.

<u>Pride</u>:   A feeling of deep pleasure or satisfaction derived from one's own achievements

"I do, Sarah, I do feel I have come a long way. Further than I ever expected to. I cannot thank you enough."

"No, Alana, I must thank you – for I can get very frustrated in my job when people kid themselves about what they bring to this room. Most only scratch the surface of their problems. It takes a brave person to delve deep and it has been a privilege to watch you work. You have worked so incredibly hard in this room."

"I know." I heard what she said and I knew it was true.

"So, now I'm going to ask you a question. Do you think you need to keep coming to see me every week?"

"Yes, definitely yes." I was shocked by the question. My Tuesdays were my saviour.

"I'm a strong believer that counselling has its place in the healing process and you have proved that but I think that there should also be a line that is drawn at the right time that says, 'I have it under my control' and for you to then fly solo again.".

I paused and thought about what Sarah was saying. It made sense but I felt a sense of panic rise up inside. What if I didn't fly? What if I slipped back to where I was? I couldn't bear to do that.

"I will still be here and available if you feel the need for a session and we'll plan the last one together. Perhaps, in two weeks time? When you came to me all those months ago, you were drowning in your own sadness. Now you are well and truly standing on firm ground. I think you will keep learning about yourself, Alana, but I will be here for back-up."

It had been a shock at first but her words were slowly making sense to me, as they always did. I was coping and I was feeling better. I had a long way to go but I <u>was</u> firm on my feet again. Perhaps, I did have the strength to go solo. I trusted Sarah. If she said I could, it was probably true. I smiled at her. "You are so good at what you do."

"Thank you, Alana."

I had been so wrong about my first impressions of this wonderful woman. Her bare feet were magnificent.

Never underestimate taking the time to really heal yourself.

CHAPTER 60

The Dinner Invitation

Eight months after my last counselling session, I was indeed flying solo. Well, not exactly flying but I was not moving in a backward direction and the dark cloud had not reappeared. I was busy working hard to build up my drama school and my girls were growing fast. Ben had wandered through my head but there had been no updates on Facebook; no emails; no texts and so I could only guess that he was still being an ostrich.

I had bought a book a few months back that had caught my eye at a service station:

'How to be Brilliant', by Michael Heppell

The title had resonated with me. I had come a long way since my darkest days but I was definitely not at Brilliant status or anywhere near it for that matter. I opened the book and saw the crisp, white pages, read the Introduction and was hooked. I had bought it with the money I would have paid Sarah Parker for the counselling session. I'd decided that I would use that money each month to keep learning about myself and that book seemed the perfect next step. I was lying on my bed re-reading a chapter about 'vision' when my phone vibrated on the bedside cabinet. I glanced across and saw it was a message from Ben. My heart thumped a bit harder and I grabbed the phone:

BEN – ALANA: "Alana, I'm sorry it's been so long. I've been sorting my life out. I'd like to ask if you would come to dinner at my house. I'd really like to talk. Ben xx.". My eyebrows raised and my eagerness to reply was burning my thumb but I breathed deeply and messaged Frankie instead.

ALANA – FRANKIE: "Ben has asked me to dinner at his home xx"

FRANKIE - ALANA: "He's got a nerve xx"

It made me chuckle. It was true. I had told a few close friends the whole, crazy, pretty distressing story about the hoo-ha that was his party. The reaction had unanimously been one of shock, disbelief and anger. They had all said, "He is out of order.", "He's crossed the line this time", "You are better than him" etc. Everyone in my close circle had thought the evening was closure for me and that it was finally time to move on.

It was true; I had been at the point of closure. I had stated to Twinkle Eyes that I never wanted to see Ben again, ever. It had been a knee-jerk reaction to a hurtful moment but it had not stopped my mind from remembering all that Victoria had said, wondering how he was every day or still believing he was the one who could make me happier than any other person on the planet.

I read Frankie's message, "He's got a nerve!" and knew straight away that she was still fuming with him for hurting her best friend. It was lucky for him he lived miles away. Otherwise, he might have been hit on the head with a handbag!

I stopped for a minute and I breathed deeply, closing my eyes. I could picture Ben clearly and tried to imagine sitting at his dinner table, eyes locked across the food and a chemistry rose up inside me out of nowhere.

It was that inexplicable magical feeling that washed over me that made me pick up my phone and reply back.

ALANA – BEN: "Long time, no speak. Thank you for the invite. I'd love to join you for dinner."

It was not what any of my sane friends would have told me to do or say. It was not what my sensible self advised me to do or say either. That was wild, crazy, loved-up, believing in 'The One' Alana talking. She had once again surfaced like the Disney Princess, and, from the bottom of the sea, came up to look for her charming prince. Although many had stripped Ben of his 'The One' label when he had treated me so inconsiderately, Wild Alana had not.

As I closed my eyes to sleep, my heart smiled. Ben Rutherford wanted to have dinner with ME.

> *Though time has passed*
> *I love you still*
> *Annoyingly*
> *I always will*

Never underestimate going back on your knee-jerk reaction.

CHAPTER 61

The Happy Ever After

The day finally arrived. Once again, I found myself driving down the motorway in a buoyant and happy mood. My mind was full of expectations; full of conversations I would start and I sang along to the Now Love Album all the way to his door.

I had never been to his house. I was imagining a huge, detached property with land and maybe a few sheep. He was a successful, well-educated and important man. I imagined his house would reflect that but as I turned into the road, I was surprised to see that the houses were not enormous. They were more compact and smaller than I had pictured. I pulled up at number 12 and smiled, as it had always been my lucky number.

I had packed an overnight bag, which I reached for as I got out of the car. I was not at all sure of the overnight invitation. It had been a complete shock two days before.

"Alana, I realise you will be driving a long way. I have a spare room which you are more than welcome to use and I'd love you to stay if you can."

It had been another one of those moments which had secured the thought that 'this' time it was happening. I had waited almost 9 years for Ben Rutherford to get his act together. I had been eager from the very first second I caught his eye as I hobbled to the church. Ben, however, had put every single obstacle and mental block in our way but on that day there appeared to be nothing in our way and it was for that reason that I had packed my overnight bag.

Ben opened the door to me and smiled a big smile. He kissed me on the cheek and ushered me in, taking my bag and coat.
"You look lovely", he said, and I felt instantly better about myself. I had not been convinced I looked lovely but Ben's words helped. I glanced around the hallway. It was not what I had imagined at all but it was a nice house, well decorated and stylish.
"Now, Alana, before you get settled in, I need to get a key ingredient for dinner. Would you mind coming with me to the shop?" He looked a little flustered.
"Of course not, let's go!" He smiled again, relieved and gave me back my coat.
We got into his car and I felt that overwhelming feeling of aliveness again. We struck up conversation straight away and off we went.

The shopping trip was a dream come true. He took my hand as we entered Sainsbury's and our eyes had locked for a second. It was magical. HE took MY hand. It was a moment to savour. There we were, in Sainsbury's, buying an important ingredient for the dinner he was going to cook for me. To the outside world it would have looked like we were a happy couple, full of the joys of love on a Saturday night. There was electricity sparking off us when we got to the checkout. I felt his body a little closer to mine and I thought I might let out a little squeal of delight but I held it in and just turned to him and smiled.

That shopping trip was the start of my Happy Ever After.

Never underestimate the magic ingredient.

CHAPTER 62

The Magic

The evening consisted of the most wonderful meal, outrageous flirting over the dinner table, followed by hours of free-flowing conversation and fun. I had been feeling nervous at first but the nerves soon diminished and we found ourselves wrapped up in the Ben and Alana magical bubble that always seemed to appear whenever we spent time together. We had both had a few glasses of wine and were laughing at a story he was telling me when he stopped mid-conversation and said:

"Alana, I can't bear it anymore. Please can I kiss you?" I did not really have time to process the question, let alone answer it, when I felt his hand on my neck and he pulled me closer. "I'm so sorry it's taken this long; I'm really happy you are here."

Then it happened. He kissed me. The man I adored, the man I worshipped and waited for, the man I compared all other men to; the man who had once been too good for me was now kissing me. I kissed him back with all the passion and love that had been stored up for him for years. The kiss lasted for a very long time. When we finally pulled apart our lips, I realised I was horizontal on the sofa and he was lying on top of me.

"I've made up the spare bed but..." There was an awkward silence, the first of the evening.

"Ben Rutherford, just kiss me", I said. We had talked for 8 years, on and off; mostly off but sometimes on. It had been the most confusing, hurtful, crazy situation but we had ended up in the right place, finally. Sparks were flying and items of clothing being removed. I was getting ever closer to the man I loved, the man I had loved for what seemed like forever.

I ran my fingers through his hair
and touched his skin
I kissed his lips
 and breathed him in.

Needless to say, the spare room was not needed.

Never underestimate the power of a happy ending.

CHAPTER 63

The Weird Goodbye

I woke before Ben. His arm was still wrapped around me and the sheets were dishevelled from the passion that had entwined us. I opened my eyes and breathed in the situation. The dream was coming true. I finally knew that he loved me as I loved him. Last night had been wonderful from beginning to end and it was continuing. Then the alarm went off.

Ben stirred from his slumber and reached over to his phone. He groaned grumpily and I snuggled into his chest comfortingly.

"I've got to be back in London by midday, so I'll have to get up and go soon." He hadn't mentioned that last night but it wasn't a bad thing. I had to get back to the girls, too. I looked up at him but his eyes were closed. I wanted to kiss him but I just looked at him instead. He looked adorable.

He opened his eyes and smiled down at me. "Right, I've got to get up." He kissed me briefly on the forehead and jumped out of bed.

"You are welcome to use the shower after me, if you want." I could sense he was rushing and I didn't want to make him late.

"It's OK, I'll have one when I get home." He looked relieved. "You jump in the shower and I'll make some tea."
He smiled and said, "Top Plan."

He left for the shower and my lips felt demoralised. No morning kiss; no waking up from a slumber good morning kiss? I felt a little cold and it wasn't the weather causing it.

I shrugged off the feeling, knowing that Ben had an important job. Being on time in his position was probably a massive pressure. He would no doubt kiss me when we had breakfast.

15 minutes later, he entered the kitchen, looking sharp, important and a little bit tetchy.
 "I don't have time for tea, Alana. I'm sorry; bit of an emergency at work; I need to get going."
I felt another pang of yearning for his kiss. Where was it? I could tell his mind was now at the office.
 "I'll get dressed quickly and then we can be on our way."
 "Sorry to rush you", Ben said, apologetically. There was still no kiss.

I rushed to pick up the debris of my outfit from the previous night, scattered on the floor, and wondered if the awful gut feeling in my stomach was due to lack of breakfast or lack of kisses from Ben. Either way, I didn't like it and I started to feel empty inside. I collected my things and got dressed in record time. I brushed my teeth and put my hair up. I looked halfway respectable for a 5-minute rush job.

Ben was all ready and waiting by the door. He gave me a smile but it wasn't a warm, passionate one like he had showered me with the night before. It was a strange smile. If I wasn't so in denial, I could have sworn it looked somewhat pitying.

"I'm sorry for this, Alana, but I do have to go." I was standing next to him, my car keys in hand.

"Don't worry, I understand. Thank you for a wonderful night last night." I smiled up at him.

"Thank you, Alana; it was wonderful to see you." Then he kissed me briefly on the lips. So briefly that it left me a little stunned.

"We'll speak soon. Have a good day."

"Yes you too, Ben." I couldn't help it. I needed to hug him. I wrapped my arms around him and felt his hand pat my back in a sympathetic way.

"Goodbye, Alana."

Never underestimate no morning kiss.

CHAPTER 64

Cold Turkey

I did not know how to process the night of the sleepover or the silence that followed. To many, it may have been a predictable sequence of events:

The crumbs were dropped
The girl rushed to pick them up
The crumbs lead to nowhere
Then the crumbs stopped

He had a proven track record for dropping crumbs. I had a proven track record for rushing to pick them up. I also had a proven track record for beating myself up for months afterwards. This beating was surely going to last an entire year.

I had asked no questions; I had put my heart in his hands; I had assumed that by inviting me to 'sleep' over, it was the start of our true love's path. I had lived the dream for a day but I had got it very wrong.

I had texted the night after we met; nothing. I texted a few days later: nothing. I texted a week later: nothing.

During that time, I lived everyday life; I fake-smiled to the world; I had conversations with my mouth while my mind was elsewhere. I was OK externally but I was sinking internally.

Why was he doing this to me? What had I ever done to him, other than love him unconditionally? Why had he dropped me from a great height twice in a year? He knew, more than ever, how I felt about him. He knew he had the key to my heart. Right then, it felt he had used the key, ransacked my mind and run away, leaving me to look at the mess he'd made and feel violated by the intrusion. What was worse was that I could feel a dark cloud looming over my head again; the cloud that had disappeared from my days was back.

"Oh, no, please, no." I shook my head when I realised I was sinking. I had been doing so well. I had finished my counselling; I was reading my 'How to be Brilliant' book and making slight progress but, faced with that hurtful rejection, I was heading back to Square One. Then, I heard a voice I hadn't heard it in a while: the Sergeant Major was back:

"You are not going to sink again. Get back up, girl." It was a strong voice and I listened, "You will not sink again, Alana."

I didn't want to sink but what else could I do? My heart was shattered again. I did not understand. Why was he not talking to me? What had I done? Then, a week later:
BEN – ALANA: "Alana, I'm sorry I haven't texted before. Hope you are OK. Have a good week. Ben x"

I had waited 168 hours for a message to make me feel better. I had felt more alone and dejected as each hour had passed. I had prayed for a text from him and there it was. It was a pointless and heartless text; it was a text to make himself feel better for not replying to me and to get me off his back. It was the pits.

I had made excuses for him all week but that text told me more than

I wanted to know. Yet again, he was fighting with his heart and his head. He loved me because he opened up his heart to me but his head did not approve. I was not the right candidate. I was not good enough.

I scanned back the night we had shared together and I searched for clues but there had been none. There had only been warmth and sparks and love. True love. Magic. The clues had only surfaced in the morning. I'd picked up on those. I read his text again and I felt heavy. There was no question, no invitation to reply to. It was a token text. Then a second text arrived:

BEN – ALANA: "Maybe we can meet in a few weeks, if you are free? x"

I could not believe my eyes. Now my heart was confused. What was that man doing to me? One minute down, one minute up. I was his yo-yo.

It was a crumb of love but it had been such an awful week, lonely and demoralising, I had to reply:

ALANA – BEN: "That would be lovely. Have a good week, too x."

Two sentences; 7 days of turmoil and anguish and all I could come up with were 2 sentences of surface chat. I annoyed myself at how easy I had made it for him. He was pulling all the strings and I was his little marionette but the attachment was better than no attachment and that deep down voice inside still knew he was 'The One'.

A few weeks calculated to just before Christmas. I found myself browsing the shops for a present for Ben. In the end, I ordered a personalised calendar of cool cars and a mug which said 'Ben Rules'. They were token gifts but I wrapped them up lovingly and made a card. I texted on the Monday:

ALANA – BEN: "Hey, Ben, just wondered if you are free for that drink. We can toast to Christmas x?"

I sent it and immediately felt I had lost any power that I possessed. Once again, my happiness was in his hands. The reply came 3 days later:

BEN – ALANA: "Thanks for the invite. I can't meet before Christmas, sorry. Enjoy the time with your family, Ben xx."

I looked at the presents I had wrapped. They were on my bedroom shelf. I shook my head and couldn't believe that, once again, I had believed in the dream. I had spent hours deciding on a gift that he'd like to open and imagined him arriving with mistletoe. How wrong could one girl be, over and over and over again?

I stood up and grabbed the two presents. I hid them in my wardrobe in an attempt to forget that they existed. It was three days until Christmas and I was not full of festive cheer. I would have to cover up the heartbreak with my increasingly good acting skills. My girls deserved the best Christmas ever. They were so amazing all year round. We had become such a tight unit. I had to put this to one side for their sakes. It would be no fun for them if Mummy was crying in the corner on Christmas Day.

So, I busied myself buying the girls' presents, making hand-made cards for all the family and watching Christmas films with the girls at night. I stayed in their room for longer than I needed to on Christmas Eve. They were both sound asleep, curled up on their sides. They were beautiful. It had been a very difficult year. I seemed to have been saying that <u>every</u> year but I had made progress. I had faced my deepest hurt and dealt with it. I had made peace with young Alana; the girl who had been unaware how unwise her choices were back then and now I was experiencing the heartbreak of Ben's rejection for the umpteenth time. What had gone right? The only thing that had gone right was the two beautiful sleeping angels in the room. I loved them and they loved me.

I knew I had saved myself from drowning by going to see Sarah Parker, but I was nowhere near a together person, I proved that with every encounter I had with Ben. I felt a peace in the room wash over me. The girls; they deserved a Mum that didn't cry alone at night; they deserved a Mum who had sunshine all around her instead of being followed by dark clouds; they deserved a Mum to look up to, not one that crumbled when a man rejected her or who depended on other people to make her happy. The two beautiful girls deserved better.

As I hugged my knees on the floor that night, listening to the deep breaths of the people I loved most in the world, a little thought crept into my head.

'Perhaps I deserve those things, too.'

There was no contact from Ben on Christmas Day. The effects of my addiction and craving for his love were hard to ignore but I survived it and Jesse and Amy showered me with love. For the first time in a very long time, I made the decision to show myself some love, too.

Never underestimate having an epiphany of who you want to be.

CHAPTER 65

Blocked

I bought a notepad and pen on 4th January 2009 and I wrote the first page of this book. I knew that I had to move on from Ben Rutherford. As true as my love was, as deep as the emotion felt, it was a vicious circle.

I thought about the garden outside Sarah Parker's safe room; how my mind had felt all twisted and overgrown and Ben's love was entangled in there, too. I had always thought it would work out, like Charles and Camilla, and at times, it had really felt like he loved me, too, but I had let it grow out of control in my mind. I had convinced myself that his love was a beautiful flower which made my life better but how do you tell a beautiful flower from a weed? Weeds can be beautiful, too, but they take over and end up ruining the idyllic garden you were hoping for.

On 31st December 2008, I emailed Ben:
"Ben, I need to know what's going on. I need to know the truth. We spent the night together; it meant a lot to me but you've been quiet ever since. I can only assume it did not mean the same to you. Love always, Alana."

"Alana, I feel so guilty about what happened. I thought I was ready. I have feelings for you but something always stops me from moving forward with you. I'm a confused man. I don't expect you to wait for me but I need time to work out how I feel. Ben xx."

It was the message that made me log into Facebook, search for his name and unfriend him. My status that day was...

"Right, that's it. I've had enough of CONFUSED people." My status attracted the most likes I'd ever had. I could hear my friends cheering from the sidelines:
"Thank goodness she's finally seen the light!"

So, I started to write the long story up until that day. Within the first few chapters, I could feel the benefits of writing it down, of seeing on paper the struggles I had faced and the behaviour I had accepted. I began to see, with clarity, that I needed to change my thinking and expect more for myself. At the same time, I completed all the exercises in 'How to Be Brilliant' and decided to take actions every day to improve my life.

I learnt how to tune into my emotions, to be aware of how I was feeling every day. I learnt how one small action in a forward direction changed everything for the better. I learnt that there were books and books of wisdom to help me become a better, stronger and less scared of the world person. I was on my way to a place called Hope. I learnt how to tap into the garden in my mind and spent time every day chopping down the weeds and tidying things up. I started to enjoy the feeling of control over my thoughts.

Gradually, the Ben weed was pulled from the ground. With each page written, a root was unearthed but I knew in my heart that he would always be important to me. I had loved him for a long time. It had not gone down the same route as a lot of true loves but it had been there all the same. I had to acknowledge that he had been a part of my life and I had loved him deeply.

I decided to purchase a garden bench in my mind. It seemed fitting to have a place to sit and think about him if I ever felt like doing so, but that he was not an uncontrollable weed that took over and wrapped me up in knots. The analogy worked for me. At first I sat there a lot but after a year went by, I was frequenting it less and less. I noticed that I was no longer the girl who cried at the end of a drunken evening with friends. I wasn't feeling tears welling up out of nowhere. I found I was capable of dreaming about the sort of life I wanted for myself and my girls and I was actively learning tools to help me.

I was still far from brilliant but I was definitely moving up the league slowly.

Then, 18 months later - 10th July 2010

BEN – ALANA: "Alana, I'm not sure if you will want to see me but I'd really like to meet up. I've got so much to say to you, Ben xx."

Never underestimate the power of writing.

CHAPTER 66

Benchmark

Frankie had been apprehensive when I first told her about the meeting I had arranged with Ben. She had watched how life had improved for me and the girls and she was worried that he would bring me down again. I loved her for caring and her concerns were also ringing in my ears, too. I had wondered whether seeing him would mess with my mind and heart but I had a point to prove to myself. I had to test what I had learnt. All the nights I had written the story of our love, I had to see if I had been successful in my quest to write him out of my head.

I spent an hour getting ready. I chose my outfit wisely so that I felt at my best. I moisturised and took time on my make-up, put my most lovely sunglasses on and looked in the mirror.

"Looking good, Alana", I said to myself. I had finally learnt how to be my own best friend. It had taken a long time but now I'd got the hang of it, it made life so much better.

I drove to the restaurant with an open mind. I had not planned a million different conversations or things I wanted to say. Indeed, I had listened to music and smiled at myself a few times in the rear view mirror. I wondered whether Ben would even recognise me. I

hardly recognised myself. I received a text as I parked the car.
BEN – ALANA: "Can't wait to see you. I'm in the bar."

I smiled but it didn't touch me in the same way. I saw him and I felt the love. I felt the butterflies and the skipped heartbeat; it was still there but there was also a lot of love in my heart already; the love I now felt for myself. I was steady on my feet and I confidently walked towards him, kissed him on the cheek, swished my long hair sassily and smiled right into his eyes.

"Long time, no see!" I beamed. I was genuinely happy to see him. He looked a little older than I remembered and I think I looked a lot better than he remembered, because his eyes sparkled brightly as he looked at me.

"Alana, you really look amazing."

I observed how I took the compliment. It was nice to hear, but I did not hang on it. I felt good and that was what mattered.

The evening was a little surreal. The chemistry, the conversation and the love still seemed to flow but I listened and looked at him in a different way. He was not on a pedestal, high above me. He was sitting right opposite me at the same height. For the first time, I felt like his equal. He skipped around certain issues, including his love life but instead of it bothering me, I just processed the information as 'interesting' and moved onto the next subject. He asked about me and I told him everything, like an open book. I had nothing to hide and I was finally heading in the right direction.

He insisted on paying the bill and I let him. After all, he did owe me for dozens of things. We left the pub and the stars were out.

"Alana, I've been wanting to say something all evening but we were having such a lovely time, I didn't want to spoil things. I have to apologise to you for everything I've done over the years. You have only ever been lovely to me and I was the opposite to you. I always had this battle between what I felt for you and the life I should be leading."

"You mean, in other words, I wasn't good enough", I said, with a smile and a raised eyebrow.

"If I'm being totally honest, that's how I felt but only because of my upbringing and short-sighted stupidness. I was being a complete twat and I hate myself for it. You are the most wonderful, generous, beautiful woman I've met and it shouldn't matter what car you drive, or where you live, I can see that now. I just wanted to say how sorry I am and ask if you can ever forgive me?" He was leaning on the bonnet of his car and he did look very sorry. His shoulders slumped and his eyes looked sad. I thought he could do with a visit to see Sarah Parker.

"I ruined chance after chance that you gave me. I now wonder what if I'd been braver to listen to my heart?"

"Well, I spent years wondering what I was doing wrong; it was hurtful. Some of those silences broke my heart. I always felt like you were out of my league, Ben Rutherford, but I'm standing here with you today and I love you as completely as I always have. God knows why but I do, but I also know that you are not good for me. I don't want crumbs of love. I want more than that. I deserve more than that. I'm a good person who went through bad things. I'm back on track now and I know what I want for myself and my two beautiful girls."

Ben looked at me "You really are amazing."

"I'm not there yet, but I'm working on it."
I smiled and believed every word I was saying. I still loved him, I still wanted to help him break out of his boxes and to be the woman he married but I knew that if I let him back in, I would spend the next 10 years trying to work him out. I had broken the cycle and it felt powerful.

"I'll always love you, Ben, and I forgive you for being a twat, which actually is quite accurate for the way you behaved at times but if it was going to happen between us, it would have happened by now

and anyway, I'm busy learning how to love myself. It's quite fun!"
He looked at me with love in his eyes.

"Alana, can I kiss you goodbye?"
I looked up at the stars and thought how romantic the scene was. Ben looked vulnerable and handsome.

I leaned over and gave him a peck on the cheek and he looked a little stunned at the quickness of it.

"Ben, we are friends now. Just good friends." I smiled and hugged him and patted his back sympathetically. "You missed the boat."
He nodded, understanding probably for the first time, how far I'd come.

"You do deserve the best, Alana. You really do." He smiled and his love entered my soul. I let it.

"I've got to go now, Ben. Thank you so much for dinner. It was lovely to see you." With that, I gave him my best smile and walked to my brand new, shiny red Suzuki Swift. In fact, it was not just a walk, it was a definite strut forming.

As we both left the car park, I was aware of his car following me to the motorway, where we would go in different directions. How appropriate that was. I was in front and he was following. He pulled up beside me at the lights and I could see him trying to get my attention. For 10 years, I had been trying to get his. As the lights turned green, I gave him a brief acknowledgement and a wave. He enthusiastically waved back and I drove off into the night.

I heard myself say out loud: "You missed the boat my darling" and I looked into the rear view mirror with a cheeky grin. It was true. He had.

On that momentous drive home, I thought about the bench in my 'mind garden', dedicated to my love of Ben Rutherford. I decided to unveil the gleaming, gold plaque that night:

*A decade of devotion to Ben
now leads me to a lifetime of love for myself
Thank you*

That feeling I drove home with; the confidence, happiness and love I felt for myself would be the Benchmark for all my future days. When I got back, I took out my journal and I drew a little doodle:

From Rut... To Strut

And a new day dawned.

Never underestimate having a benchmark for yourself.

✓ ① Maintain great relationship with the girls and family. ♡
✓ ② Maintain sistership with Frankie. ♡
✓ ③ Run a successful drama school. ♡
✓ ④ Take girls on holiday. ♡
✓ ⑤ Have a great relationship with a great pair of shoes. ♡
✓ ⑥ Read a book. ♡
✓ ⑦ Write a book. ♡
✓ ⑧ Go to a Spa. ♡
✓ ⑨ Be happy. ♡
✓ ⑩ Find myself. ♡

It's time to write a new list!

♡ Alana :)
x

I'd love to hear your thoughts on the book. If you would like to contact me my email is: jlwbenchmark@gmail.com or visit my website www.jlwbenchmark.com.

My wish is that you... **never underestimate yourself.**

Joanna Louise Wright

xxxx

Made in the USA
Charleston, SC
22 June 2015